Site 22

The RV Mysteries - Book FOUR

L. D. KNORR

MILFORD
HOUSE

an imprint of Sunbury Press, Inc.
Mechanicsburg, PA USA

MILFORD HOUSE

an imprint of Sunbury Press, Inc.
Mechanicsburg, PA USA

For information about special discounts for bulk purchases, please contact Sunbury Press Orders Dept. at (855) 338-8359 or orders@sunburypress.com.

To request one of our authors for speaking engagements or book signings, please contact Sunbury Press Publicity Dept. at publicity@sunburypress.com.

ISBN: 978-1-62006-144-2 (Trade paperback)

Library of Congress Control Number: 2019951176

FIRST MILFORD HOUSE PRESS EDITION: October 2019

Product of the United States of America
0 1 1 2 3 5 8 13 21 34 55

Set in Bookman Old Style
Designed by Crystal Devine
Cover by Lawrence Knorr
Edited by Lawrence Knorr

Continue the Enlightenment!

Chapter 1

"Mrs. Tolliver, this is Helen Moran." "Why hello Helen! I do hope you have some good news."

"Yes I do, Mrs. Tolliver. I've located Twinkles!"

"Oh thank God! Is he all right?"

"He's just fine. I'll bring him back to your place in about ten minutes."

"Is he at the house on Rothman Drive we talked about?"

"No, not exactly. I'll tell you all about it when I bring him home."

"Well, Ok! I'll be waiting out front Helen!" Mrs. Tolliver said in excitement.

Mrs. Tolliver appeared at the Moran Investigations Agency office a day earlier in a state of extreme distress. Her male Lhasa Apso, named Twinkles, had been missing for three days and she was absolutely sure some evil dognapper had stolen him.

Helen had the eighty-something white-haired senior citizen sit down in the red leather chair facing her desk and obtained pertinent information on Mrs. Tolliver's beloved Twinkles.

"Mrs. Tolliver, do you have a photograph of Twinkles?"

"Yes, I do," Mrs. Tolliver replied as she produced a four by six photo of a small, brown and white, long-haired dog, with a black button nose. "He's a Lhasa Apso."

"What makes you think that Twinkles was dognapped?" Helen inquired.

"I had let Twinkles out the back door and into the yard to do his business and when I went to let him back into the house he was nowhere to be found. I noticed the gate in the fence was open and I saw a strange white van turn the corner down the street. I had never seen that van in the neighborhood before."

"I see. Has Twinkles ever run off?"

"No he never ran off, but he did pay a visit to Wilma Henson's poodle, Phoebe, across the street about a month ago."

"How did he get out of the yard at that time?"

"The gas man accidentally left the gate open when he read the gas meter."

"You said he paid Mrs. Henson's poodle a visit. Is Twinkles neutered?"

"Oh no, I never had the heart to have that done to him."

"I see. Have you checked with Mrs. Henson to see if Twinkles paid her Phoebe another visit?"

"Yes I did, but she said she hadn't seen him."

"Hmm, does Twinkles have a collar on?

"He has a collar with an I.D. tag, but I took it off when I gave him a bath. I forgot to put his collar back on when I let him out into the yard to do his business."

"So, at this moment he has no collar or I.D. on him?"

"Oh my, I'm afraid that's so!"

"Mrs. Tolliver, has anyone contacted you for a ransom demand?"

"No. No one has called yet," Mrs. Tolliver replied.

"Mrs. Tolliver, our agency fee in cases like this is one hundred and fifty dollars per day. We can set a time limit of three days. If after that time we haven't located Twinkles, you can decide if you want us to continue searching. We will call you with a daily report and also call you immediately if we have reliable information as to Twinkles' whereabouts."

"That sounds fair enough to me. He means the world to me since my husband Harold passed two years ago and I would do anything to get Twinkles back."

"Ok, Mrs. Tolliver, I'll get busy right away and try to find him."

"Oh, thank you very much, Mrs. Moran. Please find him!

"We'll do the best we can, Mrs. Tolliver. Oh, and please call us immediately if Twinkles should happen to come back home on his own accord."

Helen wasn't knowledgeable of all dog breeds so when Mrs. Tolliver left the office she researched the Lhasa Apso breed on the internet. She learned the Lhasa Apso is a one-thousand-year-old breed that originated in Tibet and served as sentinels in Buddhist monasteries.

After her research on the breed, Helen checked the on-line yellow pages for the location of the Kenner Humane Society. She thought it unlikely that Twinkles was dog-napped and was most likely found, and since he was not wearing a collar, turned over to one of the area's animal shelters. She had an hour before the Humane Society closed and headed there without delay in her blue Honda CR-V.

The teen filling in at the Humane Society's front desk didn't know if they had received a Lhasa Apso. In fact, he was not sure what a Lhasa Apso looked like. When Helen showed him a picture of Twinkles he was still not sure if they had received that particular dog. He said there are a few small long-haired dogs back in the kennel and that she was welcome to check.

Helen went through the door leading to the kennels and started a slow walk past the first row of pens. She no-ticed all of the dogs had access to an outdoor run through a small opening covered with hanging plastic strips. The inside area of the kennel was air conditioned but still warmer than the front office. The animal odor was strong but bearable. She passed two pens with small hairy dogs but neither one looked like Twinkles. As she started up the second row she spied a small, hairy, brown and white dog. But when she compared it to the picture of Twinkles she could see that the color pattern was no match. The sign on the front of the pen stated that this particular dog had been there for over a week. Twinkles is only missing for three days. The rest of the dog runs produced no candidates for Twinkles.

Helen decided to head home as the other two shelters in the area would already be closed for the day. She planned to get a fresh start in the morning on her quest to find Mrs. Tolliver's beloved pet.

Hank, Helen's husband and agency partner, arrived home as she was preparing dinner in their Kenner Louisiana home, which also serves as the headquarters of the Moran Investigations Agency. The agency office addition to their home was completed the previous year. Hank is a retired detective from the Kenner, Louisiana police force. Upon his retirement, the couple purchased a Fleetwood Bounder motorhome and had a few harrowing adventures in the unplanned investigations of homicides while on the road. A year and a half ago, shortly after acquiring his State of Louisiana P.I. license, he solved the murder of a furniture store owner whose body Hank's grandson, Chip, snagged on his fishing line. The following month Helen obtained her P.I. apprentice license and recently passed her P.I. exam. The agency's business has grown steadily over the past year leaving little time to enjoy their motorhome.

"I took on a new client today, Hank."

"That's great! What's the nature of the case? Hank questioned.

"Mrs. Melba Tolliver hired us to find her missing Lhasa Apso named Twinkles. She suspects he was dognapped, but I believe he just happened to run off to a nearby rendezvous or was taken in by someone."

"I see. What in heck is a Lhasa Apso?"

"It's a small long-haired breed that originated in Tibet," Helen replied.

"Well, I hope you can wrap it up before the weekend. We need to leave on Sunday, as planned, to make it over to Charleston in time."

The planned trip to Charleston, to see the Fourth of July fireworks display at Patriot's point, had been in the works for three weeks. They took a break from the agency's business to enjoy a much-needed excursion in their neglected motorhome.

"I should be able to find Twinkles in a day or two. I checked out the Humane Society late this afternoon with no luck. I'm going to check two more shelters in the morning and then if he isn't being held, I'll start canvassing the neighborhood. I nearly forgot to ask how your case is going."

"I'm sure I'll close it out tomorrow. I found out today that Missy Braddock has been involved with a local golf pro who left for Ohio two days ago to play in a PGA tournament. She bought a ticket for the same flight as his. I'll probably spot her in the gallery on Saturday on the golf channel. I just need to find out which hotel she's staying at and break the news to her husband, Paul. That should close the case."

"All right!" Helen replied. "I can't wait to go on that trip. We really need to get away for a while. The Bounder has been just sitting out there in the driveway for three months now. The poor thing will think we abandoned it."

The next morning Helen reproduced half a dozen copies of Twinkles' picture on her photo printer and set out to check the two remaining animal shelters. On the way, she stopped back at the Humane Society and left her card and one photo, and requested them to call her if they took in a dog that looked like Twinkles.

Her visits to the other two animal shelters in the area produced negative results as well. If someone found Twinkles and saw he had no collar I.D., they might have taken him in. A worse thought was an auto struck and killed him on the street. A call to Kenner's Public Works Department verified they had not picked up any small dog carcasses in the last week.

Helen returned home to grab a quick lunch before setting out again on her quest to find Twinkles. A thought occurred to her as she sat in the kitchen eating a BLT on toast. When she finished her lunch she called Mrs. Tolliver who answered the call immediately.

"Mrs. Tolliver, this is Helen Moran. I need to ask you a question."

"Yes, what is it, Helen. Have you found Twinkles?"

"No, not yet, but I need to know if you take Twinkles on long walks around your neighborhood."

"Why yes, I do."

"Do you have a specific route that you take on those walks?"

"Yes, I usually walk up my street then circle around Mouton and Rothman Drives and then back down my street. Why do you need to know this?"

"I suspect Twinkles might have caught the scent of a female in heat and set off to pay her a visit like he did with Mrs. Henson's poodle. When was the last time you took him for a walk?"

"It was the morning before he disappeared."

"Did he act funny as you passed any of the houses on your walk?"

"I don't understand. What do you mean by acting funny?"

"Did he sniff the air a lot and try to pull you toward a certain house?"

"Hmmm, yes, come to think of it he did! It happened up on Rothschild Drive."

"Great, Mrs. Tolliver! Do you remember which house it was?"

"I don't remember the house number, but it was the big two story house with all the columns. It was on the side of the street that has sidewalks. Rothman Drive is very short. You should be able to find it."

"I'm heading right out there, Mrs. Tolliver. I'll call you back if I have any luck."

Helen turned into the golf course community where Mrs. Tolliver lived and followed her GPS unit to Rothman Drive. It didn't take her long to find a stately two-story house with a row of columns that spanned the first and second floors. The house was unique in the neighborhood so she pulled up into the driveway and proceeded to the front door. A small dog started to bark when she rang the doorbell.

A middle-aged woman with shoulder-length brown hair dressed in white shorts and a yellow tight-fitting tank top answered the door. "Yes, can I help you?"

"I hope you can," Helen replied. "My name is Helen Moran from the Moran Investigations Agency. I am trying to locate a small brown and white male Lhasa Apso that has been missing for a few days. I was wondering if you have seen this dog in your neighborhood."

Helen produced the picture of Twinkles for the woman to look at.

"The dog must be very valuable in order for someone to hire a detective agency to find it," the woman replied.

"I don't believe he is very valuable, only greatly loved."

"If the dog is loved so much, why is it running around without a collar or I.D.?"

With that statement, Helen knew she came to the right place. How could she know Twinkles was without a collar if she hadn't seen him? "His name is Twinkles and he was let out into the owner's back yard to do his business shortly after his bath. He escaped out of the yard before his collar could be put back on," Helen responded.

"Well, Detective Moran, Twinkles did stop by here a few days ago. He appeared at our backyard fence while my neighbor and I were lounging out at the pool. Josephine, my female Shih Tzu was inside the fence. She is in heat and your Twinkles tried his hardest to get through the fence to her."

"Great! Do you know where Twinkles is now?" Helen excitedly asked.

"My neighbor thought he was a stray because he wasn't wearing a collar. She took possession of him and was going to take him to a shelter, but she since became hopelessly attached to him. He's still right next door. I'll call her and let her know you're searching for him. I have been feeling uneasy about him living right next door since he seems to have a twinkle in his eye for Josephine."

"Thank you, Mrs. . . . I never did get your name."

"I am Emily Lacobee and my neighbor's name is Caroline Hebert. If you want to wait inside, I'll call Caroline and have her bring Twinkles over."

Helen waited in the foyer which was as big as her own living room. It had a vaulted ceiling two stories high topped with a skylight. She could hear Mrs. Lacobee talking on the phone but she could not make out what was said. A short time later Mrs. Lacobee returned to the foyer and said, "Caroline wants you to meet her out in front of her house. She'll have Twinkles with her."

"Thank you for all of your help Mrs. Lacobee. You've been very kind."

"I'm very curious Detective Moran. How did you know to knock on my door?"

"Twinkles' owner, Mrs. Tolliver, was walking Twinkles through your neighborhood and she remembered that he seemed overly interested in your house. He must have detected that your Josephine was in heat."

"I see. Oh, there's Caroline out front waiting for you."

"Thanks again Mrs. Lacobee."

Helen walked the short distance to the front of a large one-story brick house. Mrs. Hebert was waiting on the top of the front steps holding the leash of a small brown and white dog.

"You must be Mrs. Hebert," Helen said as she approached the steps. "I am Helen Moran."

"Hello Mrs. Moran, Emily said you are a private detective."

"Yes, I am, Mrs. Hebert. From Moran Investigations," Helen replied as she displayed her official P.I. badge."

"Business must be slow for your agency if you are searching for lost dogs," Mrs. Hebert said.

"No, it is quite to the contrary, Mrs. Hebert. We were in the process of wrapping up a wayward person case and planning a little vacation when Twinkles owner, Mrs. Tolliver, stopped by our office. The poor elderly lady was so distraught that I couldn't turn her away."

"Before I turn him over to you, I want to make sure this is the dog you are searching for."

Helen pulled the picture of Twinkles from her purse and compared it to the dog sitting obediently by Mrs. Hebert's side. "All of the markings match exactly, including the star-shaped pattern on his head," Helen said as she showed the picture to Mrs. Hebert.

"I guess that star shape on his head is why he was named Twinkles," Mrs. Hebert said while perusing the photo.

"That is correct, however, it seems he also developed a twinkle in his eyes for every female dog for a mile around," Helen replied.

"Twinkles!" Mrs. Hebert said in a commanding voice.

Twinkles immediately stood up and looked up at Mrs. Hebert.

"Well, I guess it's him. Here, you better take him before I change my mind." Mrs. Hebert said in a reluctantly sounding tone while handing the leash to Helen."

"I can see why someone would become attached to him," Helen said. "He sure is a cutie pie and seems very well behaved. Oh, I just remembered. Yesterday, in my search for Twinkles, I stopped in at the Humane Society. They are holding a very cute little brown and white dog that looks a lot like Twinkles, except for a few differences in the markings. They are looking for someone to adopt it into a good home."

Mrs. Hebert's sad look turned into a smile and said, "I was always reluctant to have a dog, but since Twinkles arrived I've had a change in attitude. Thank you for the information. I'll head down there tomorrow morning and have a look."

"Well, I better get Twinkles back to Mrs. Tolliver," Helen said. "I'll be sure to tell her he was well taken care of, Mrs. Hebert. And good luck tomorrow morning. Oh, I'll bring your leash and collar back as soon as I drop off Twinkles. You may need them in the morning. C'mon Twinkles."

Helen walked Twinkles to her Honda and he jumped right up into the front seat when she opened the passenger side door. She called Mrs. Tolliver from the car.

Mrs. Tolliver was waiting out front when Helen pulled into the driveway five minutes later. When Twinkles saw Mrs. Tolliver through the car window, he became very excited, rapidly wagged his tail, and tried to paw his way through the window to get to her. Helen reached across and opened the passenger door to let Twinkles out and he ran right into the arms of Mrs. Tolliver who received an enthusiastic face licking.

"Where did you find my naughty little boy?" Mrs. Toll-iver asked.

"It seems he had an amorous eye for a female Shih Tzu at the house you mentioned. The next door neighbor took him in and that's where I found him," Helen explained. "I highly recommend that you keep a very close watch on your little lover boy"

When Helen returned home after returning Twinkles to Mrs. Toliver, and the leash and collar to Mrs. Hebert, she saw Hank in the driveway checking the engine compartment of their motorhome and asked, "Is the Bounder ready to hit the road?"

"Everything looks good engine wise. The sewer hose looks a little worse for wear," he replied. "I better run over to the camper store and pick up a new one. Then we'll be ready to load up and hit the road."

"Did you locate the wandering Missy Braddock?"

"I did. She booked into the Hilton right near the golf course. I called her husband, Paul, and gave him all of the particulars and oddly enough he didn't seem all that upset. I have a feeling that he's glad he now has sufficient cause for an upcoming divorce. He told me a check for my fee will be in the mail today."

Helen replied, "Since you mentioned checks, I just deposited one in our account from Mrs. Tolliver. She even added a little bonus for finding her Twinkles so quickly."

"That's great! That should cover our gas bill for the trip," Hank said. "We should send Twinkles a thank you card. Let's pack up tomorrow and be on the road early on Sunday morning. That should give us plenty of time to make a leisurely trek over to Charleston. We should have enough time to explore the town before next Friday's fireworks."

"I can't wait, big guy, sounds like a plan," Helen replied.

Chapter 2

Hank and Helen hadn't ventured out in their motorhome for over three months so they divided the trip into three easy driving days to reach Charleston. The first day's distance was the longest being four hundred miles to Thomasville, Georgia. It was a direct shot on Interstate 10 to Tallahassee, Florida and then a short drive up to the Ochlocknee Plantation RV Resort north of Thomasville. Helen had wanted their first stop to be Biloxi. She had a large plastic casino cup half full of quarters hoping to play the slots at one of the casinos but agreed to only stop to top off the Bounder's gas tank along Interstate 10.

They pulled into the Ochlocknee campground late in the afternoon, stopped at the designated area for registration and walked into the quaint office.

"Good afternoon folks. Welcome to our campground. My name is Ruth. How can I help you?

"Good afternoon, Ruth. We have a reservation for one night. I am Hank Moran and this is my wife, Helen."

Ruth checked the reservation log on the computer and said, "Ah yes, here you are." And after taking a glance out the window she asked, "You are driving the gold and black Bounder?"

"Yes ma'am, we are."

"Beautiful motorhome! Hmm, I'm afraid there is only one site left that will accommodate your rig and that is site 22."

"It sounded like you said that with a little apprehension. Is there something wrong with the site?" Hank asked.

"Oh, no," Ruth replied. "It's a perfectly good site and one of the most spacious in the campground. I am sorry I gave you the wrong impression."

"No need to apologize, Ruth," Helen responded. "Please don't mind my husband. He's a retired police detective and is sometimes overly suspicious. I am sure site 22 will be just fine."

"Very well then," Ruth replied. "That will be thirty-four dollars. Do you wish to use the same credit card as on your reservation?"

"Yes please," Helen answered.

After processing the payment Ruth circled their site on a campground map and drew red arrows for directions to it. "I'm here by myself this afternoon; otherwise I would escort you to your site. It's not hard to find. Just take the next right and its a few sites down the circle drive. The sites are plainly numbered. Just follow the map."

"I'm sure we will have no trouble finding it," Helen replied.

A few minutes later Hank stopped the Bounder in front of site 22 and unhitched the Honda CRV. It was a large-sized site and he had no problem backing the Bounder into it. Helen parked the CRV to one side as Hank connected the Bounder up to the sites 50-amp electrical console.

As he was opening the package for the newly purchased sewer hose, he noticed an elderly couple across the drive observing his set-up procedure. The woman pointed in his direction and said something to her husband but Hank could not make out what she said. He just waved to them and busied himself with the chore of connecting the remainder of the utilities and TV cable. He looked back towards the couple's site but they had already gone back inside their huge fifth wheel trailer. Their site looked like it was a semi-permanent one with wooden steps and yard ornaments.

He thought maybe the woman had pointed to something wrong with the Bounder, but after a quick walk-around inspection he concluded they were just admiring his motorhome.

With his hookup chores completed, Hank entered the coolness of the Bounder to wash up before dinner. Helen was preparing a chef's salad of tomatoes, lettuce, cucumbers, green peppers, and onions.

"How did you know I was salad hungry?" Hank said as he passed by on the way to the bathroom.

"I figured you would be hungry for just about anything I would make. I brought the leftover ham and chicken along. Which one do you want on your salad?" Helen asked.

"I'll take the ham with ranch dressing," Hank responded.

Helen replied, "Good, I wanted the chicken."

"If you wanted the chicken why did you ask? You said I would eat anything you make," Hank said with a chuckle.

"Oh, I just wanted to make you feel that you had a choice," Helen answered.

Hank continued on to the bathroom, shaking his head with an amused look on his face. He had noticed a change in his wife of over thirty years from a dutiful housewife to a more assertive partner since she acquired her P.I. license. He enjoyed watching how Helen eagerly absorbed all of the new dimensions in her life.

After dinner, they watched a TV show about a famous female psychic where they had believers and debunkers debating her abilities. The show was just about over when Hank said, "When I was back on the force, did I ever tell you about the case of the dwarf psychic that held up the First National Bank in Kenner?"

"No, you didn't dear. Really? A dwarf psychic?" Helen answered.

"Sure was. We had an APB out for a small medium at large."

Helen let out a groan and tried to stifle a laugh, but with the timing between the TV show and Hank's rare attempt at humor, she failed.

The next morning Helen arose first, put the coffee on, opened the blinds, and peered out the kitchen window at the orange tinted sunrise. It was then she noticed the distelfink she had hanging in the kitchen window was missing. She had purchased the Pennsylvania German good luck charm up in Lancaster County, Pennsylvania, on a previous road trip. She searched the top of the counter and the floor thinking it might have fallen from the window while on the road, but could not find it. Then she remembered it was still in the window when she prepared last night's dinner.

She was about to call for Hank to ask him if he removed the distelfink when she felt a cold chill in the forward section of the Bounder. Hank came out of the bedroom before she called for him.

Hank noticed the perplexed scowl on Helen's face and asked, "Is the coffee ready, Sunshine?"

"You don't get any coffee until you tell me what you did with my distelfink," Helen gruffly replied.

"What are you talking about?"

"The distelfink is missing from the window and I can't find it anywhere."

"Helen, I didn't touch the distelfink. It probably fell off the window and slid under the table or something."

"I looked all over the kitchen floor for it and can't find it," Helen replied.

Hank bent down to look for the distelfink under the dinette. When he straightened back up he noticed it hanging in the opposite window just above the dinette. "Ahem, please look in the window above the dinette," he said.

"How did it get over there? Helen questioned wearing a confused look and wrinkled brow.

"You probably moved it there and forgot," Hank answered.

"Hank Moran, I did not move the distelfink to that window and I am not suffering from dementia!"

"Ok, Ok, I believe you. I know I didn't move it there and if you didn't do it, it must have been some little elves overnight.

And why is it so cold in here? Did you reset the thermostat?"

Helen replied, "I didn't change the thermostat, I also noticed a cold chill in here and thought you changed it."

"Well, I didn't change it," Hank replied. I'll go check it."

Hank checked the thermostat in the hall and said, "The thermostat is set on seventy-five, right where it should be."

"I'll tell you what" Helen replied. "I really don't feel like cooking breakfast this morning. They are serving a community breakfast down at the main hall for only a small donation. Why don't we go do that and then get on the road?"

"Good idea," Hank replied. "All this mystery has made me hungry."

"When aren't you hungry?" replied Helen. "For the life of me, I don't understand how you can keep eating what you do and not be overweight."

"Must be good genes," Hank replied with a smile.

Hank and Helen detected the enticing aroma of breakfast cooking as they walked toward the main hall. Once inside they joined the line of hungry campers as they filled their plates with pancakes, sausage links, and scrambled eggs. Coffee was served from a large urn at the end of the buffet.

Hank and Helen sat across the table from the elderly couple who had the permanent site across the drive from them. Their names were Harry and Wilma Schultz and during the friendly conversation, Helen found out they hailed from Pennsylvania.

"We were up in Lancaster County a short time ago," Helen said. "We really enjoyed touring the Amish country. Hank was introduced to shoofly pies and bought three to take back with us. I bought a small distelfink and hung it in the kitchen window of our Bounder for good luck."

"Did it work?" Wilma asked.

"So far, so good, except for one thing," Helen replied. "Oh. What was that?" Wilma asked.

"Well, it seems the distelfink mysteriously relocated itself from our kitchen window to the window above the dinette. I tried to blame Hank for it but he insists he didn't move it."

On hearing Helen's comment about the distelfink Harry and Wilma looked at each other with raised eyebrows and Wilma said, "Well, Helen. You are in site 22."

Hank immediately looked up and asked, "What does site 22 have to do with a self-relocating window ornament?"

"We have been in the site across from number 22 for over five years now and we have heard about some strange things happening over there," Wilma replied.

"What kind of things?" Helen asked excitedly.

"People have had things moved around the campsite. Some have heard noises at night right outside their motorhomes, and a few have heard a light tapping on the outside walls, but upon checking, nothing was found."

"It was probably just raccoons," Hank replied.

"That's what we would like to believe," Wilma replied. "However, this is the first we heard about something being moved inside a camper. Some people even claim the site is haunted."

"Aha, I knew Ruth down at the office acted a little suspiciously when she assigned us that site," Hank said with a chuckle.

"Well, Ruth always makes it a point to use site 22 only when the campground is booked full," Wilma replied. "It works out well for us as we don't have to look across the lane and see neighbors most of the time."

"Well, we plan on pulling out right after breakfast, so you'll have your unobstructed view back shortly," Hank said. "And hopefully we'll leave the raccoon or whatever it is behind to pester someone else."

"It's been nice meeting you folks and we wish you a safe trip," Wilma replied, as Hank and Helen excused themselves from the table to continue their journey.

One hour later Hank and Helen were back on Rt. 84 heading for their next stop near Jesup, Georgia which is approximately halfway to Charleston from Thomasville. The one hundred and fifty-mile leg of their journey took a leisurely three hours and they arrived at the Morse Landing Campground in the early afternoon.

Harriet, the clerk informed them that check in time wasn't for another hour yet, but she would bend the rule a little bit since they weren't very crowded.

Hank thanked her for her kindness as the transaction for a site was completed.

After setting up the Bounder Helen suggested they take a ride around town in the hope of finding a roadside vegetable stand. As they were motoring down the Savannah Highway towards Jesup, Helen spotted the Jesup drive-in theater.

"Hank look, a real honest-to-goodness drive-in theater and it looks like they're still in business! Let's go tonight!"

"Are you serious?" Hank replied. "You want to spend over two hours cooped up in the Honda when we could lie in bed and watch a movie in the Bounder?"

"When was the last time you went to a drive-in movie? Do you realize this must be one of the last drive-ins still in operation in the country? We have to go now that we have the opportunity!" Helen implored. "And besides, the Honda seats do recline."

Hank drove past the marquee and noticed "The Expendables 2" was playing. "Well, ok, let's go. I guess I could endure a Bruce Willis flick," Hank replied.

"We can even park in the back row and get a little frisky,"

Helen suggested.

"What, and interrupt my movie?" Hank replied, earning a sharp elbow jab to his side.

"Hey, that hurt," he uttered.

"I'll make it up to you tonight, in the back row of the drive-in," Helen replied with an impish grin.

A mile farther down the road they spotted a vegetable stand and purchased fresh tomatoes, sweet onions, leaf lettuce, and a few jalapenos.

Later that evening, after thoroughly enjoying their drive-in movie experience, they both felt the now familiar chill as they entered the motorhome.

"Something has to be wrong with the air system," Helen stated.

"I'll check it again," Hank replied in exasperation.

Hank checked the thermostat and thermometer in the hall which both registered seventy-five degrees. After a quick walk-through, he noticed the temperature once again felt comfortable throughout all areas of the Bounder. He put his arms around Helen and said, "Everything seems OK. In fact, it felt really comfortable back in the bedroom. Why don't we go back there and finish what we started at the drive-in?"

"That sounds like an offer I can't refuse?" Helen replied.

Early the next morning as Helen was about to enter the kitchen to start a pot of coffee, she caught a fleeting glimpse of what she thought was a teenaged girl in the forward area of the Bounder. She stopped dead in her tracks and called out, "Who's there," but received no reply.

She immediately did an about face and hurried back to the bedroom as Hank was stirring.

"Hank, wake up, wake up!" she shouted in a state of high anxiety.

The tone of her shout registered on Hank and he quickly sat up and asked, "What's the matter!?"

"I just saw someone in the front of the Bounder! It looked like a teenaged girl!" Helen replied.

Hank quickly arose and slipped on a pair of jogging pants.

"Stay back here while I check it out," he said as he started barefoot up the hall but Helen, not wanting to miss anything, was right behind him.

Hank made his way slowly through the kitchen and living area to the front of the motorhome feeling a chill in the air but seeing no one. Upon checking the entry door he turned and said, "This door is still locked from the inside. No one could have gotten in, and we would have heard the door close if someone had just left."

"I know I saw someone," Helen stated firmly.

"I hate to mention it again, but did you notice the slight chill near the cockpit?" Hank asked.

"No not this time. Don't forget I was behind you," Helen replied. "But I do have a major case of the goosebumps."

"I better get that pot of coffee started," Helen said as they retreated back to the kitchen.

It was then she noticed the distelfink was once again missing from the kitchen window. She abruptly turned and spied it where it was once again hanging in the window above the dinette.

"Hank look, the distelfink was moved again!"

"Looks like we brought the raccoon along with us from the Thomasville campground," Hank replied.

"What the heck is going on, Hank? That was surely not your raccoon I saw this morning. And your raccoon would not be moving my distelfink around!"

"While you get the coffee started I'm going to get my running shoes on and jog down to the office for the morning paper," Hank said. "What you need is your daily crossword puzzle to ease your mind and take it off distelfink mysteries."

As Hank entered the campground office he was greeted by Harriet who had just opened for business.

"Good morning, Mr. Moran. You're up early this morning."

"Morning, Harriet. Just stopped in for the daily paper," Hank replied as he pulled one off of the pile at the end of the counter.

"I hope you are having a pleasant stay at our campground," Harriet said. "It's a shame you can't stay for more than one night."

"We'd like to stay a little longer but we want to make it over to Charleston for the Fourth. And if we move a little faster we might leave behind the little gremlin that's been plaguing us."

"Oh. Having trouble with your rig?" Harriet asked.

"No. No trouble with the rig," Hank replied. "But we have had some strange things happen the last two days."

"I don't mean to be nosy but what kind of strange things?" Harriet asked.

"Oh, things like a window ornament being move from one window to another, an occasional strange chill in the air, and my wife's claim she saw someone inside the motorhome this morning," Hank replied.

"Oh my! If someone broke into your motorhome we should call the sheriff."

"That's ok; we are positive that no one broke in. I think that my wife was mistaken."

"Well, it sounds like y'all picked up a mischievous hitchhiking spirit," Harriet replied with a chuckle.

"Like I said, maybe we'll get lucky and leave it behind us. We'll be checking out in about two hours," Hank said as he laid a dollar on the counter for the newspaper and made his way out the door.

Back in the Bounder, Hank related his brief conversation with Harriet to Helen.

"Hank, maybe Harriet was right about us picking up a spirit. It could have happened back in the Thomasville campground at the site we had. After all, Wilma Schultz did say some people thought the site was haunted. I'm going down to the office and talk with Harriet."

As Helen went out the door all Hank uttered was, "Good grief!"

Helen entered the campground office as Harriet was finishing up another newspaper sale to a small elderly silver-haired lady wearing a pink jogging suit. "Good morning, Mrs. Moran. What can I do for you?"

"Good morning Harriet. My husband Hank was just here and he mentioned his conversation with you about the strange things that have been happening in our motorhome. You mentioned that we might have picked up a spirit."

"Oh, Mrs. Moran, I was just joking of course."
"Well Harriet, I think there might be something to what you said," Helen replied. "It all started back in the campground near Thomasville. A couple that we had breakfast with mentioned that some people thought the site we were in was haunted."

"I don't know what to tell you, Mrs. Moran. I haven't had much experience with things of that nature," Harriet replied.

The elderly lady in the pink jogging suit, who was listening intently to the conversation spoke up, "Mrs. Moran, I'm Jenny Wright. I couldn't help but hear what you just said. My brother Earl and his wife Arlene had the same thing happen to them in their motorhome. They actually had a priest perform an exorcism to rid them of a spirit."

"You know, Mrs. Moran, I just remembered something," Harriet said. "There is a psychic that lives in Jesup that one of my campground customers went to see about a year ago. I recall the psychic told her things about her dead brother that only his sister would know."

"Oh, her name is Betty Hamilton," Jenny said. "She's a single mother that lives over on Plum Street. I was thinking about calling her myself. I was hoping I could contact my dead husband to see if it was alright to marry again. I have her number in my trailer if you want it."

"You bet I do!" Helen replied without hesitation.

"Well then, follow me!" Jenny replied excitedly.

On the way to Jenny's trailer, Helen found out that Jenny was eighty-three years old and fell in love with a seventy-six-year-old widower she met at the senior center in town.

Jenny related, "My friends kid me about robbing the cradle, but I need a younger man who can keep up with me."

Hank was just finishing his cup of coffee when Helen came bursting through the door of the Bounder with her cell phone to her ear.

"Hello, Ms. Hamilton?"

"Yes, who's calling please?"

"My name is Helen Moran. I got your number from a lady named Jenny Wright at the Morse Landing Campground. She said that you may be able to help us with our problem."

"What problem do you have, Mrs. Moran?"

"My husband and I are traveling in our motorhome and it seems we may have picked up a . . . umm . . . presence at the last campground we stayed at."

"What makes you think that, Mrs. Moran?"

"Well, for one thing, I have an ornament that I hung in the kitchen window above the sink and it keeps being moved to the window on the opposite wall. This morning I am sure I saw a teenaged girl inside the motorhome, but no one was there when my husband checked. Also, we keep feeling chilly spots in the motorhome."

"It sounds like you may be correct about a presence."

"Ms. Hamilton, would it be possible for you to come to the campground and do an investigation, or whatever it is you do, and find out what we have in our motorhome."

"Yes, I can, Mrs. Moran. I am extremely curious as to why a spirit would want to go for a ride in your motorhome. I have never run across this before."

"Oh thank you, Ms. Hamilton. We are at the Morse Landing Campground in site number eleven. It's the black and gold Fleetwood Bounder."

"I can be there within the half hour, Mrs. Moran."

Hank and Helen were sitting outside on their site's concrete patio, and rose, when a white Toyota SUV stopped in front of the Bounder. A young woman emerged who was extremely pretty with short brown hair, wearing snug-fitting jeans and a white top.

"She sure doesn't look like a medium," Hank said to Helen as the woman approached.

"Mrs. Moran? I'm Betty Hamilton."

"Yes, hello Ms. Hamilton. This is my husband, Hank."

"Hello, Mr. Moran. I heard what you said when I got out of my car. I'm sorry I left my turban and crystal ball back at the house," she said with a smile.

Slightly embarrassed and red-faced, Hank had no immediate reply.

"Mr. and Mrs. Moran, before we start, I want to tell you a little about myself. To begin with, I don't charge for my services. I first became aware of my gift as a young girl. As

I grew up I began to realize that I was given this gift to help departed soles, who have lost their way, to complete their journey to the other side. I am writing a book about my experiences and if your case proves to be worthy, I would like to include it."

Hank replied, "Ms. Hamilton, we wouldn't stand in the way of including our case in your book, but I do have a request. We would like to approve the final draft of our part in it before it is released."

"Yes, of course, Mr. Moran. Shall we get started?"

"Yes, please," Helen replied. "But first, let's not be so formal. Please call me Helen."

"Thank you, Helen, and please call me Betty. You mentioned on the phone that there was an object being moved inside your motorhome?"

"Yes, it is a small distelfink charm that is hanging in the kitchen window. We have found it numerous times in the window above the dinette."

Betty replied, "Since the entity seemed to handle the charm, I need to hold it in order to enhance contact."

"Oh, please do!" Helen replied.

"Ok. If you will kindly wait out here, I need to go into the motorhome alone."

"Be our guest," Hank replied with a sweeping hand towards the door.

Hank and Helen sat on the sites picnic table as they watched Betty Hamilton occasionally pass by the windows in the Bounder for the last ten minutes.

"It looks like she is talking to herself," Hank said.

"Or maybe she is talking with our uninvited guest," Helen replied.

"Do you really think we have a ghost in our motorhome?" Hank asked.

"Hank, there is definitely something strange going on and the presence of a spirit is the only answer."

"Well, we'll soon find out. It looks like she is coming back out."

Betty Hamilton emerged from the motorhome with a huge smile on her face.

"You're smiling. You must have good news," Hank said.

"It depends on one's perspective," Betty replied. "What's good news to me may not be good news to you and Helen. You do have the spirit of a teenaged girl in your motorhome."

"I was right! I knew I saw a young girl," Helen replied. "Why did she pick our motorhome?"

"You were parked in site 22, the same site her parents had their motorhome parked in and she noticed your sign," Betty replied.

"What do you mean our sign?" Hank inquired.

"The Moran Investigations sign on your motorhome's door," Betty replied. "Let's sit down and I'll explain it all to you."

When they were seated at the table Betty Hamilton continued her account of what happened inside the Bounder.

"To begin, there is only one spirit in your motorhome. Her name is Sarah. She was murdered at the campground near Thomasville. She never saw the person or persons who murdered her. Her parents are still grieving and she wants closure on the case for their benefit. She needs to do this before she can continue her journey to the other side."

"How are we supposed to help?" Helen asked.

"She is hoping that you two can solve her murder," Betty replied.

"Oh boy, here we go again!" Hank uttered in exasperation.

"Why is it that every time we try to go on a peaceful RV trip, we wind up in a murder investigation."

"It's because we're lucky," Helen replied. "This could prove to be a lot more interesting than watching a bunch of fireworks."

"You got me there," Hank replied,

"Betty, when did her murder happen?" Helen asked.

"She doesn't know," Betty replied. "Spirits have no awareness of time like we do in the physical world. "It could have happened last week or twenty years ago."

Hank replied, "When we felt those chills in our motorhome I didn't think it was going to be this type of cold case."

"It looks like we'll be taking our passenger back to Thomasville," Helen said.

"I am sure that once you return to the campsite, Sarah will leave your motorhome," Betty said. "Here is my card. I hope you will keep in touch with me. I would be very interested to hear if you decide to pursue the case. I am willing to help in any way that I can."

"Thank you, Betty, you've been a big help already. We'll be sure to keep in touch," Helen replied.

"Oh, Mr. Moran, Sarah says that the Ochlocknee campground has Fourth of July fireworks," Betty said as she rose to leave.

"There you go!" Helen responded.

"How did she know about the fireworks," Hank mumbled to himself.

Chapter 3

As soon as Betty Hamilton left, Helen pulled out her cell phone and tapped on the number for the Ochlocknee Campground in the phones directory. After the fourth ring, a woman answered and said, "Ochlocknee RV Resort, would you hold please?"

Helen assumed the clerk was in the middle of registering an arriving camper, so she paced impatiently around the picnic table until the clerk came back on the phone.

"Sorry if I made you wait, can I help you?"

"Yes, this is Helen Moran. We decided to head back to your campground and need a reservation for a week. We would like site 22 again if at all possible."

"Oh hello, Mrs. Moran this is Ruth. I am delighted to hear you are returning to our campground. Let me check on that site for you. We are starting to fill up for the long Holiday weekend."

After a short pause Ruth came back on the line, "Mrs. Moran, since you will be staying a week, I can make site 22 available for you."

"Thank you, Ruth, we will be arriving later this afternoon."

"May I ask why you want site 22?" Ruth inquired.

"It was the site we had the other day and we just liked it, that's all."

"I was just wondering. Wilma Shultz, the lady across the drive from that site, mentioned that you had a little problem there," Ruth replied.

"Oh, it turned out to be no problem at all, Ruth. Oh, by the way, was there a murder of a young girl there at the campground sometime in the past?

"Why yes there was about ten or eleven years ago," Ruth replied.

"Do you happen to recall her name?" Helen inquired.

"Mrs. Hartman, the campground owner mentioned it to me when I first started working here. If I remember correctly I think her name was Sarah," Ruth replied.

Helen responded excitedly, "Thank you, Ruth, see you soon," and ended the call.

Hank had secured loose items inside the Bounder in preparation for the road when Helen came in.

"Okay we have a reservation for a week in site 22," Helen said excitedly. "And guess what? There was a murder of a teenaged girl named Sarah about ten years ago at the campground."

"Unbelievable," was all that Hank replied.

"I'll finish the inside and do the slides. Why don't you go out and unhook the utilities," She said to Hank. "And let's not forget to call the Charleston campground to cancel our reservation.

"Yes ma'am," Hank responded. "You sure seem in a hurry to get tied up in another investigation. Are you sure you want to get involved?"

"C'mon, Hank, It's going to be fun."

"I didn't think it was much fun when you got kidnapped by that Michigan militia the other year," Hank responded.

"No, that wasn't much fun, but because of our adventure up there in Michigan, and your saving Senator Westbrook from drowning, we got invited to dinner at the White House."

"In my mind, the dinner at the White House was very minor compared to your escaping unharmed from those idiots up there," Hank responded.

"This time I promise I'll stick very close to you big guy. C'mon, we have a passenger who needs our help."

"Ah yes, the passenger. Here we go again," Hank replied.

Three hours later they pull into the Ochlocknee RV Resort and stopped to register. Hank and Helen both walked into the campground office and Ruth greeted them once again.

"Mr. and Mrs. Moran, it's good to see you again. I have you scheduled for site 22 for one week. We will be having live music and fireworks Friday night to celebrate Independence Day."

"Sounds great Ruth," Helen replied. "How much do we owe you for the week?"

"Our normal weekly rate is two hundred and twenty-five, but since the Holiday is included I have to increase it to two fifty."

"That's no problem, Ruth. Here's my card."

After Helen signed the credit slip she asked, "Ruth, do you know anything else about the murder of the girl that happened here ten years ago?"

"I don't know much more than what I mentioned to you on the phone," Ruth replied.

"We are private investigators and we understand the person responsible for the murder was never found. We are here to look into the case," Helen replied.

"Wow, that's exciting. I'm sorry I can't be of any more help to you."

"That's OK Ruth. Is it at all possible for us to talk with Mrs. Hartman?"

"I am sure you can. She lives in the cottage back behind this office. She enjoys talking with the campers. She drives a big old blue Chrysler. If it's parked in her driveway she's at home."

"Thanks' Ruth. We'll walk back and pay her a visit after we get set up."

"OK then," Ruth said. "You already know the way to your site. Hope you have a great stay and if you need anything just call the office. We are here from eight till six. And good luck with your investigation."

"Thanks, Ruth, we'll stop by if we need anything."

As Hank was hooking up the black line hose he looked up across the drive and saw Harry and Wilma Shultz sitting in lawn chairs on their small concrete pad watching him. He gave them a friendly smile and a wave and they returned the gesture. After hooking up the fifty amp power cord, water hose, and TV cable line, he entered the Bounder to see if Helen needed help with the slides. The main slide was almost fully extended and the bedroom slide started.

"I see you have everything under control in here," Hank said.

"All you need to do yet is turn on the air conditioner. It's awfully warm in here," Helen replied.

"I assume then there are no mysterious cold spots," Hank replied with a chuckle.

"I haven't felt any cold areas and my distelfink is still in the right window."

"Could it be that our passenger already left the building?"

Hank responded.

"We'll see," Helen answered. "Are you ready to go have a talk with Mrs. Hartman?

"Soon as I wash up a little," Hank answered.

Harry and Wilma were still sitting out when they started their walk to Mrs. Hartman's cottage.

Wilma waved for them to come closer and said, "I see you're back. Weren't you on your way to Charleston?"

"We were but we had a change of plans. We liked it here so much we decided to come back and stay a while." Helen answered as she took Hank's arm to keep him walking.

Once they were out of earshot Hank said, "Wasn't that just a tad rude?"

"I didn't want to get drawn into a long conversation about the reason for our return. And I'm trying to avoid telling anyone that we had a spirit in our motorhome. You know how people are. They'll think we're a little whacko. Also, I wanted to keep walking because I'm anxious to hear what Mrs. Hartman has to say."

Numerous campers were sitting out and gave them a friendly wave as they walked by. The campground was already filling up with kids on bicycles and skateboards. As they approached the cottage situated behind the office they noticed a light blue vintage Chrysler with the signature fins sitting in the driveway.

"Wow, that sure looks in great shape!" Hank exclaimed. "It must be from the early sixties."

"It's a nineteen-sixty-one Newport," came a voice from up on the cottage's porch.

Helen took the few steps to the front of the porch and saw an elderly lady wearing a Georgia Bulldogs sweat suit seated in a wooden rocking chair.

"Are you Mrs. Hartman? Helen asked.

"Yes, I am." The lady replied.

"I am Helen Moran and that is my husband Hank admiring your car."

"My husband Ronald gave me that old Chrysler as a wedding present. He passed on twenty-one years ago. I keep it in tiptop shape in his memory. I've had many offers from people wanting to buy it but I can't part with it," Mrs. Hartman replied.

"Mrs. Hartman, do you have a few minutes to talk?" Helen asked.

"My manager Ruth called and said you might be stopping by. You and your husband are the private investigators wanting information on the death of that poor girl back in two thousand and three. What is it you need to know?"

"Well, you just answered my first question," Helen replied. "Do you happen to know the exact date?"

"Yes, I do. I remember it because it happened on the Fourth of July. It was on a Friday night just like this year."

"Hmm, that's very interesting," Helen replied. Wanting to verify Betty Hamilton's findings, Helen then asked, "Do you remember the girl's name?"

"Her name was Sarah Payne. She was a real-pretty dark-haired girl about seventeen or eighteen years old. She came here camping with her parents just about every year at this time.

They told me that was the last year they would be together because Sarah was starting college in the fall."

"Oh, that is so tragic! It turned out that it WAS their last year together," Helen replied.

"Yes, her parents were heartbroken, to say the least."

"I understand the police ruled Sarah's death as a homicide and that the person responsible was never caught. Is that still true?" Helen asked

"Yes, that's still the case. May I ask why you and your husband are investigating that girl's death?" Mrs. Hartman asked.

"We've been asked to look into it by someone we would like to keep anonymous at this stage," Helen replied.

"Since you asked Ruth specifically for site 22, you probably already knew that Sarah's parents were in that same site when the tragedy occurred?"

"Yes, we found that out this morning," Helen replied.

Mrs. Hartman looked questioningly at Helen and then commented, "Some people claim that Sarah's spirit is still seen down by the lake and that strange things happen at site 22. Mind you, I've never seen anything myself, but every now and then a camper claims they saw what looked like an apparition of a teenaged girl."

"Mrs. Schultz mentioned something to that effect when we were here the other day," Helen replied. Trying to change the subject Helen then asked, "Do you remember where Sarah's parents live?"

"Yes, they are from up in Athens,"

"Athens? That's where the University of Georgia is. Since they said it was their last year together, apparently Sarah must not have enrolled there," Helen said.

"You are very perceptive Mrs. Moran. They said she was accepted at one of the old Ivy League schools up north, but I no longer recall which one."

Helen detected a slight scowl on Mrs. Hartman's face when she mentioned a northern school.

Hank, who was listening intently to Helen's questioning of Mrs. Hartman, decided not to interfere and just take notes. If there were any remaining questions in his mind, he would ask them when Helen was finished.

"Did Sarah's death occur during the day or was it at night?" Helen inquired.

"A group of teenagers found her body down by the lake late at night," Mrs. Hartman replied.

"Please tell us what you remember about that night."

"Well, the campground was filled to capacity as it always is for the Fourth. In the past, we hired a local country band for entertainment, but that year we tried a rock band. We usually have a lot of teenagers for the holiday so we thought it would be a good idea to keep them entertained. The rock band played extremely loud. I considered it a bunch of noise myself, but the teens loved it. I am sure they heard it over in Grady County. The band played for an hour and then took a break during the fireworks display. They played again until about ten thirty. I was sitting just where I am now when I heard shouting down by the lake. A teenager then ran up to the porch shouting for someone to call 911 as there was a girl's body down by the lake."

"What time was this?" Helen asked.

"It was some time after ten thirty," Mrs. Hartman continued. "Eleven was supposed to be the start of the quiet time in the campground, but obviously that never would happen. After I called 911, I went down to the scene and saw a woman, who I later found out was a nurse, performing CPR on a girl's body. A sheriff's deputy arrived and when he saw the girl he called Sheriff Rainey. The nurse had no success in reviving the girl. When the EMT's arrived in the ambulance they also tried, but also without success. The sheriff had arrived right behind the ambulance. The coroner arrived shortly thereafter. After the coroner officially pronounced the girl dead Sheriff Rainey called in a request for two more deputies as they had a campground full of people to question. As it turned out, nobody actually heard or saw what happened. I imagined that even if the girl screamed she would not have been heard over the noise from the rock band."

"Where were Sarah's parents during all of this?" Helen asked.

"When I realized who the girl was, I looked around and saw that her parents weren't at the scene. I told Sheriff Rainey what site they were in and he went to their motorhome to inform them. They were sitting out on their pad watching all the commotion not realizing their daughter's misfortune was the cause of it. Mrs. Payne collapsed when she heard the news and was taken to the hospital in the ambulance."

"Have Sarah's parents ever returned to the campground since their daughter's death?"

"No, they have never come back. According to Sheriff Rainey, they sold their motorhome."

"Does Sheriff Rainey still hold the office?"

"No, Jim retired five years ago. Shiloh Berry is now the sheriff."

"I see. Does Mr. Rainey live in the area?" Helen asked.

"He has a place in the country just up the road near Merrillville. He and his wife Alma dropped in to visit about a year ago and he was still fretting over not being able to solve the girl's murder."

"It sounds like he might welcome some help with the case," Helen said. "Has the new sheriff ever been in contact with you about it?"

"No, Sheriff Berry seems to have no interest in something that far back in time."

"Well, I think we have taken up enough of your time, Mrs. Hartman. Hank, do you have any questions."

"Only one more question, Mrs. Hartman. Do you happen to have a record of all of the registered campers for that weekend?" Hank asked.

"Yes, I am sure I still have the log book for that year. Sheriff Rainey borrowed it for his investigation, but he had later returned it. It should be in one of the storage boxes in the back room of the office."

"We may want to look at it, or better yet, would it be possible to obtain a copy of the registration pages for the week leading up to and including July 4, 2003?"

"I'll have Ruth make the copies for you. If you stop by the office tomorrow afternoon she'll have them ready for you."

"Thank you, Mrs. Hartman. And thank you for all of the information," Hank said.

As they walked back to the Bounder Hank said, "It looks like we sure got our work cut out for us."

"I know," Helen responded. "Where in the world do we start?"

"We have to interview the previous sheriff and then try to get a copy of the case file from the present sheriff, Shiloh Berry," Hank answered. "Obtaining the file may not be easy. We need the names of the rock band members and the names of the campground employees that were present. That information will most likely be in the case file. If not we'll have to go back and ask Mrs. Hartman."

"What about checking newspaper archives," Helen asked.

"It might be worthwhile to get more background information before we really dig into the case."

"That's a good idea," Hank said. "Depending on how good the reporting was, there might be useful information in the articles that aren't in the police case file. Sounds like a good place to start."

"Newspaper archives are usually available at the public library. I'll give them a call," Helen said.

Helen's call to the Thomas County Public Library confirmed that archived editions of the Thomasville newspaper are available on microfilm for the period around the murder. "The library opens up at nine tomorrow morning. Let's get there when it opens," Helen said.

"After our visit to the library, we can grab an early lunch, and then pay a visit to former sheriff Rainey," Hank added. And just maybe he'll put in a good word for us with Sheriff Berry."

Chapter 4

The next morning Hank and Helen were waiting outside the front door of the Thomas County Library when an elderly lady unlocked the door at nine o'clock sharp.

"Good morning, may I help you," said the matronly lady, her hair worn in a bun, and looking at them over a pair of wire-rimmed reading glasses. Hank thought that if she was the guest on the old *What's My Line* TV show, he would immediately guess she was a librarian.

"We're here to do research with your newspaper archives," Helen answered.

"Follow me and I'll show you how to use the reader. What is the date you are researching?" the librarian asked.

"Starting on July 5th, 2003 and the following two weeks for a start," Hank answered.

"OK, if you wait here by the reader-printer I'll be back shortly with the film."

Helen had noticed the nameplate "Mrs. Fritch" on the librarian's desk as they passed by. When the librarian returned with the roll of film Helen asked, "Are you Mrs. Fritch?"

"No, I'm Mrs. Weston. Mrs. Fritch is attending a seminar up in Atlanta today. I'm just filling in for her."

"I'm Helen Moran and this is my husband Hank. We're researching the murder of a girl that happened up at the campground back in 2003. I was wondering if you recall it."

"I'm sorry I don't. I only moved into the area three years ago. It's too bad Mrs. Fritch isn't here. I am sure she would remember it."

Mrs. Weston loaded the roll of film into the reader. "Now, all you have to do is press the forward or reverse buttons on the right depending on which direction you want to move. This machine is also a printer. Just press the print button if you want a copy of what is on the screen. Copies are twenty-five cents each."

"Thank you, Mrs. Weston. I think we can handle it from here," said Helen.

Hank brought up the front page of the Saturday, July 5th, 2003 *Thomasville Times*. The headline read:

"ATHENS TEEN MURDERED AT OCHLOCKNEE CAMPGROUND"

The corresponding article to the headline contained basically the same information as they had obtained from Mrs. Hartman. The reporter's name who wrote the article was Jason Hicks. Hank recorded the name in his notebook.

The Sunday paper was the next edition and the only article on the murder was an interview with the campground owner, Mrs. Hartman. She was perplexed that a thing such as murder could take place in her family-oriented campground.

The article in Monday's edition was basically a blurb from Sheriff Rainey stating that numerous leads were being followed and the department was doing everything it could to bring the murderer to justice. The reporter, Jason Hicks, questioned the sheriff about the safety of the town with a murderer running loose. The sheriff gave his assurance the citizens in the town were safe because he strongly believed the murder of Sarah Payne was an isolated incident.

Reporter Hicks then asked if it was possible the murderer was a fellow camper who was just in town for the

holiday weekend and subsequently left the area. Sheriff
Rainey stated that it was a distinct possibility the murderer was no longer in the area.

Hicks' next article was in Friday's edition and contained a short interview with Sheriff Rainey. Rainey stated
that a number of local suspects were cleared and he was
still following a few leads.

No other articles on the murder of Sarah Payne were
found during the two-week requested period.

"Well, that wasn't much help," Hank said in resignation.

"Do you think it would be worthwhile to check later
editions?" Helen asked.

"We already know the case was never solved so I doubt
there would be anything useful in later papers," Hank responded. "Our time would be better spent contacting ex
Sheriff Rainey and talking with him. We can come back to
the library later if need be."

"I would like to come back and have a chat with Mrs.
Fritch the librarian," Helen said. "I am sure she must know
all of the gossip surrounding the murder."

"OK, we'll add Mrs. Fritch to the list," Hank responded.
"Now, let's give ex-sheriff Rainey a call to see if he is open
to a visit."

Helen accessed the white pages on her cell phone and
found a listing for Jim Rainey. She pressed the call icon
and a man said "Hello" after the fourth ring. She set her
phone on the speaker function so both Hank and she
could listen and talk.

"Hello, sir. Is this Mr. Jim Rainey?" Hank inquired.

"Yes, it is. Who's calling?"

"Mr. Rainey, I am Hank Moran from the Moran Investigations Agency. Could you spare the time to talk about a
cold case that happened when you were Sheriff of Thomas
County?"

"It depends. What case are you referring to?"

"We are investigating the Sarah Payne murder that occurred eleven years ago at the Ochlocknee Campground."

There was a momentary silence and then Rainey spoke, "I'm not familiar with your agency. Are you from the area and why would you be looking into that particular case?"

"Our office is located in Kenner, Louisiana. We are investigating the case at the request of a client who wishes to remain anonymous."

"Kenner, Louisiana huh? You're a long way from home Mr. Moran. Not being familiar with your agency, how do I know you're legitimate?"

"Mr. Rainey, I can understand your skepticism. I am a retired robbery/homicide detective with thirty plus years on the force. I can give you the number for the Kenner Police Department. Please call and ask for Captain Benson. He or anybody in the Investigative Services Bureau will vouch for my legitimacy."

"I have their number up on my computer, Mr. Moran, and your number on my caller I.D. I'll call you back in ten minutes."

Hank was about to say thank you but realized Rainey had already disconnected the call.

"Do you think he'll call back?" Helen asked.

"I'm willing to bet he will," replied Hank. "Mrs. Hartman said Rainey was still fretting about not being able to solve that case. After he checks us out I am sure he will come around and help all he can."

Hank was starting to worry that after fifteen minutes Rainey had not called back. "I wonder why he's taking so long," Hank muttered.

"Give him a little time dear," Helen said. "He and Captain Benson are probably trading war stories."

Five more minutes passed and Helen's phone finally rang. She handed it to Hank to answer it. "Moran Investigations, Hank Moran speaking."

"Mr. Moran, Jim Rainey calling you back. I did check you out with the Kenner Police Department. Captain Benson seems to hold you in high regard. After his glowing reference, I googled your name and read about your exploits in the last couple of years. You have been quite busy solving murders, saving a Senator from drowning, and receiving a big award from the president."

"I do like to keep busy in my retirement, but sometimes things get a little out of hand, Mr. Rainey."

"Well, Mr. Moran, if you want to stop by the house we can talk about the Sarah Payne case. How about in one hour."

"We'll be there Mr. Rainey. We have your location on our GPS. If we get lost we'll call."

"That's fine, see you in an hour."

With the call ended, Hank said, "Well, we have an hour to kill. What do you say we get some lunch."

"Good idea. There's a barbecue house a few blocks away on Smith Street," Helen said after searching for restaurants on her phone.

Envisioning a juicy barbecue Hank said "That search program sure is great. Let's go."

The GPS system said they had reached their destination as Helen spied "The Raineys" written in bold white lettering on a large black mailbox at the end of a long tree covered driveway. Hank turned the Honda into the driveway which led to a small but elegant antebellum home.

Ex-sheriff Jim Rainey rose from a front porch rocker as they exited the Honda and approached.

"Mr. Rainey?" Hank said as they stepped up onto the porch.

"That's me," Rainey said. "I see you had no trouble finding my place."

"No trouble at all. I'm Hank Moran and this is my wife and agency partner Helen Moran."

After shaking Hank's hand, Rainey took Helen's hand and said, "So I get to meet the lady who made that brave escape from a nasty militia group up in Michigan. It's a pleasure to meet you, ma'am."

"It's a pleasure to meet you too sir," Helen said.

"Why don't y'all have a seat here on the porch and we'll get down to business. I understand someone hired your agency to look into the Sarah Payne murder?"

"That is correct, sir," Hank said. "At this point in time, our client's name must remain confidential. If we are successful in solving the crime, the client's name will be revealed."

"Sounds kind of mysterious, but I guess I can live with that," Rainey said.

Helen thought, "If he only knew how mysterious it actually is."

"What do you know so far?" Rainey asked.

"As of now we have gathered background information on the case," Hank answered. "We have talked with Mrs. Hartman at the campground and reviewed newspaper articles at the county library. We are ready to dig deeper into the case and that is why we requested to talk with you."

"I see. I guess it won't hurt to have fresh eyes look at the case. Well, there's no better place to start than the beginning," Rainey began. "911 was called at 10:40 the night of July the fourth. One of my deputies was in the area at the time and responded to the call. When he arrived at the scene an off duty nurse was performing CPR on a teenaged female. My deputy noticed the bruises on the girl's neck and proceeded to call me. I arrived on the scene just behind the ambulance. The nurse had since given up on the CPR before I arrived. The ambulance crew also began CPR but also with negative results. My deputy and I had trouble keeping people back from the scene which was by then fully trampled upon. We sealed off the area and told everyone to wait at their campsites as everyone in the camp was to be questioned. As the coroner arrived, Mrs. Hartman realized who the girl was and didn't see her parents in the area. She informed me that her name was Sarah Payne and her parents were in site 22. There was nothing more to do at the scene until the coroner had finished his work so I walked up to their site to inform them of their daughter's death. When I arrived at site 22, I saw a middle-aged couple sitting out on their pad apparently just watching all the commotion."

Although Helen had heard the account from Mrs. Hartman, she still gasped at the thought of Sarah's parents sitting out, watching all the activity, and not knowing their daughter was the source of it all. "I can't even imagine how they felt when you informed them of their daughter," Helen said.

"It was one of the hardest things I had to do in my whole time as sheriff," Rainey continued. "When I confirmed they were Mr. and Mrs. Payne, I told them of their daughter's death. Mrs. Payne stood, screamed, and immediately collapsed. I called my deputy on the radio and told him to send the ambulance up to the campsite. I told Mr. Payne that he should accompany his wife in the ambulance as there was nothing he could do here. He protested, but when I told him the coroner was in the process of removing his daughter's body he relented and climbed into the ambulance."

"What condition was the girl's body in?" Hank asked.

"The nurse who first performed CPR said the girl's body was still warm to the touch. That is why she performed CPR. The back of her head had been cut and bruised. There was a partially embedded rock in the ground next to her head that had a large amount of blood on it. Her shorts were removed and her underpants were torn. The coroner determined during the autopsy that she was sexually assaulted with bruising in the vaginal area. Condom lubricant was found with no trace of semen. He also

determined the blow to the back of her head was not fatal
but enough to render her unconscious. The actual cause
of death was asphyxiation due to strangling. There was
also a small trace of marijuana in her system."

Hank offered the following scenario: "It sounds like she
was attacked and thrown to the ground, her head hit the
rock knocking her unconscious and then raped. I would
guess she awoke during the rape, started to scream, and
was strangled to keep her quiet."

"That was what we surmised also," Rainey said.

Helen asked, "How could all of that happen with a
camp full of people? This place is not that big."

"Well Mrs. Moran, there would have been people in
the immediate area during the fireworks display. After the
fireworks, the rock band started its final set. From the information we gathered, the young people went to the stage
area for the music and the adults disbursed to their campsites. The area then would have been fairly deserted."

"Did the questioning of all the people in the campground produce anything worthwhile," Hank asked.

"Our questioning provided nothing of any help. A few
people saw one of the rock band's guitar players named
Beasley, walk with Miss Payne down to the lake to watch
the fireworks, but he was up on the stage playing when the
assault occurred."

"What about Miss Paynes' actions after the fireworks
were over? Did she stay in the lake area or did she follow
the rest of the teens to the stage? Helen asked.

"When we questioned Beasley he said he asked Miss
Payne to accompany him back to the stage area, but she
said she wanted to sit by the lake and think for a while.
She told him she was worried that she had made the
wrong choice for college and wanted to sort things out in
her mind."

"Is there any possibility that Beasley could have left
the stage during the band's last set?" Hank asked.

"Not according to the other band members," Rainey replied. "They claimed that he played the entire forty-five-plus minutes of the set."

"Could you give me the exact timeline of the evening? When the band played and when the fireworks started and ended?" Hank asked.

"Yes, according to Mrs. Hartman, the band's first set was from eight to eight forty-five. They announced that the fireworks would begin at nine, which they did right on time. The fireworks lasted approximately twenty minutes and the band started its last set shortly after nine thirty. They played till about ten twenty."

"Who actually discovered the body," Helen asked.

Rainey replied, "After the band quit, a small group of teens went down to the lake, supposedly to party. A girl named Jennifer Higgins saw Miss Payne first and thought she was asleep. One of the boys approached her to ask if she wanted to join them. He shook her and then noticed the blood on the ground around her head and her partial nakedness. One of them ran up to the office and told Mrs. Hartman to call 911."

"Did anything of significance turn up in the subsequent investigation?" Hank inquired.

"If we uncovered anything of any importance we wouldn't be sitting here this afternoon discussing the case," Rainey replied. "It turned out to be a dead end case with no witnesses, no fibers, and no suspects. The medical examiner did find a few pubic hairs on her body but with no usable DNA"

"Were there any other similar crimes in the area before or after the Payne case?" Hank asked.

Rainey replied, "We checked for prior crimes and there were a few rapes in the five years leading up to the 2003, but we couldn't relate any of them to the Payne case. We apprehended a guy that had committed two rapes in a two-year period afterward, but the suspect was proven not to be in the area at the time of the Sarah Payne murder."

"How is your relationship with Sheriff Berry?" Hank asked.

"We are on cordial speaking terms although I wouldn't consider him to be a close friend," Rainey replied. "Why do you ask?"

"I was hoping that you could pave the way for us to have a look at the case file," Hank replied.

"That won't be necessary," Rainey replied. "Before I left office I made a copy of everything in the file with the intent of someday solving the crime. I am sure that Berry had added nothing to the file since. You are welcome to borrow it if you promise to return it in the same condition. And I want you to keep me informed of your progress. I am also willing to help in any way I can during your investigation."

"By all means, we would like to borrow your file, Mr. Rainey and we would gladly welcome your assistance," Hank said.

"Well, now as long as we will be working together let's not be so formal. Please call me Jim."

"And likewise, we are Hank and Helen," Hank replied.

"OK, let me go get the file so you two can get to work," Rainey said.

Rainey went into the house and returned a few minutes later with a file type clear plastic storage container and set it on the porch floor. "You will find the entire file organized so please try to keep it that way. There are reprints of the crime scene and autopsy photos and also some notes and thoughts I had written after I left office."

"Ok, Jim. We'll treat the file like it was our own and return it in a few days," Hank said as he picked up the container. "We are going to swing by Sheriff Berry's office as a courtesy to let him know what we're up to. Does he know you have a copy of the case file?"

"Yes he does," Rainey replied.

"Is it okay if we mention that we talked with you?" Hank asked.

"He's an easy going fella. You can tell him of my involvement," Rainey replied. "Oh, one more thing Hank, I am still very curious as to the name of your client."

"Jim, you will be the first to know when we can divulge it," Hank replied as he and Helen stepped off the porch to leave.

As they drove away from Rainey's house Helen called the campground on her cell phone. Ruth answered on the other end. "Ruth, this is Helen Moran. Do you have the copies ready of the registration book that we requested from Mrs. Hartman?"

"Yes, I do. Stop by the office on your way in. It's all ready and waiting for you," Ruth replied.

"Thank you for your help, Ruth. I would like to make an additional request if it is not too much trouble. When all of the campers that are coming for the July 4th Holiday have checked in, I would like to get a copy of this year's registration also."

"Well, the 4th is on Friday, so most everyone with reservations should be checked in by Thursday evening. I can copy it for you then," Ruth replied.

"That will be perfect, Ruth. I really do appreciate your help."

"That was a very good idea," Hank said when Helen was off the phone. "You want to compare the two copies to see if any of the campers coming this year were also present eleven years ago."

"You got it, partner," Helen replied.

"Ok, while you have your phone handy, call Sheriff Berry's office and see if he can spare a few minutes out of his busy schedule for us," Hank requested.

Helen had already added the Thomas County Sheriff's Department number to her list of contacts. The switchboard operator answered on the second ring.

"Thomas County Sheriff Office, how can I help you?"

"This is Helen Moran from the Moran Investigations Agency. I'm calling to see if Sheriff Berry could spare a few minutes to talk with us. We are conducting an investigation in the county and would like to give him a heads up on our activity."

"I'm sure he can. Let me transfer your call, Ms. Moran."

"Thank you," Helen replied.

Less than a minute later Sheriff Berry came on the phone, "Sheriff Berry speaking."

"Sheriff Berry, my name is Mrs. Helen Moran from Moran Investigations. We are conducting an investigation in the county and would like to have a short meeting with you to discuss it. Could you spare a few minutes this afternoon?"

"If you are in the area you can stop in now. I need to be in a meeting at the county commissioner's office in an hour," Sheriff Berry replied.

"We can be there in ten minutes," Helen replied.

"That will be fine Mrs. Moran," Berry replied. "By the way, I got a call from Jim Rainey and he said you folks were ok."

"That was very kind of him," Helen replied. "See you in ten minutes."

Chapter 5

After a few words with the receptionist, Hank and Helen were shown to the office of Thomas County Sheriff Shiloh Berry. Sheriff Berry was seated behind his desk and rose to greet his visitors and shake hands. He was over six feet tall with brown hair and green eyes and in his late thirties. Helen was surprised to see how young the sheriff was and handsome too.

"Mr. and Mrs. Moran, I'm Sheriff Berry. How can I be of service to you?"

"We are looking into a cold case in the county and as a courtesy we wanted you to be aware of our activity," Hank said.

"Jim Rainey mentioned that you are conducting an investigation of the Sarah Payne murder. What brings you all the way over from Louisiana to look into that case?" Berry asked.

"We have a client who asked us to investigate it, and since we are in the area in our travels we agreed to the request," Helen answered.

"Jim mentioned about that mysterious client who wishes to remain anonymous. Why all the mystery?" Berry asked.

"The name of our client will be revealed upon the successful conclusion of our investigation. Until that time the client will remain anonymous," Helen answered.

"Well then, as Jim might have told you, the case is as cold as Boston in January. At Jim's request, I read over the case file when I took office five years ago and put it right back into storage. I figured that if Jim couldn't get anywhere with it when it happened, it would be a waste of time re-opening it. I know Jim had worked very hard on the case and he still obsesses with it today."

"I am a retired robbery/homicide detective from the Kenner Police force and I know how it feels to have one unsolved case haunt you," Hank replied. "It's always there in the back of your mind."

"I reckon I can see how that could happen," Berry said. 'That girls murder was the biggest thing to happen in the county back then and nothing like that has happened since. I think Jim just feels like he left the people down by not bringing the murderer to justice."

"Just so you know, we borrowed Jim's copy of the case file. Was there anything added to the file after his retirement?" Hank asked.

"Nothing has been added. Jim's copy of the file should be as complete as the original."

"Could you share any thoughts that you might have had when you read over the file?" Helen asked.

"Well, the main thought I had was that, in a crowded campground, I couldn't believe there were no witnesses to the crime," Berry replied.

"I had the same thought," Helen said. "We are hoping that some of the campers that were here eleven years ago come to this year's celebration. If we're lucky we might get a chance to interview them and perhaps scare up knowledge of a witness."

"Well folks, I have to get to that meeting in the commissioner's office. If you need the help of the sheriff's department just give me a call and I wish you luck in your investigation."

"Thank you, Sheriff. We'll keep you informed if anything breaks in the case," Hank said.

As they walked back to the Honda Helen said, "I think it was nice of Jim to give Sheriff Berry a call and pave the way for us."

"Yes, it was. I get the feeling that Jim is excited to get help on the case after all the years," Hank said. "Sheriff Berry said that Sarah Payne's' murder was the biggest thing to happen in the county. Jim Rainey's department might not have had the expertise to handle it back then."

"You might be right, but it sounds like he really tried," Helen said.

On the way into the campground, Hank stopped in front of the registration office to pick up the copy of the camper registration pages for the Fourth of July period of 2003. As they entered the office they were greeted by a young man with the obvious attributes of Down syndrome, who said, "Welcome to Ochlocknee Campground."

"Eddie is our official greeter for the Fourth of July holiday," Ruth said. "Eddie Parks is Mrs. Hartman's grandson and we have the pleasure of his help every year at this time."

"Hello Eddie, I am Helen Moran and this is my Husband Hank."

Hank shook hands with Eddie and said, "Glad to meet you, Eddie." Hank was mildly surprised at Eddie's strong firm handshake.

"Mr. and Mrs. Moran are private investigators," Ruth said.

"Like on TV?" Eddie excitedly asked with big eyes and raised eyebrows.

"Yes, like on TV," Ruth replied.

"Wow, are you here to find some bad guys?" Eddie inquired.

"We're here to find out what happened to a young girl named Sarah, many years ago, here at the campground," Helen answered.

"Oh, I must go and help Gramma now," Eddie said as his happy demeanor suddenly changed. He promptly turned and hurried out of the office by the back door.

"Did he just get upset when I mentioned Sarah's name?" Helen asked.

"Oh, sometimes he has abrupt mood changes like that. He has a very short attention span," Ruth answered downplaying Eddie's reaction.

"Hmm, well anyways, we just stopped in to pick up the copies of the two thousand and three July fourth camper registrations."

"I have them right here," Ruth responded as she handed the printout to Helen. "I'll have this year's copies ready for you tomorrow night."

"Ms. Ruth, would you happen to keep a record of when a camper leaves. What I mean is, eleven years ago, would you have noted if someone left the morning after the murder?" Hank inquired.

"I am afraid that wouldn't be in the records Mr. Moran," Ruth replied.

Helen thanked Ruth for her assistance and as they were heading out the door Helen's cell phone rang. She tapped the answer icon and said hello.

"Hello, Helen, this is Betty Hamilton. I'm just calling to see how you are making out with your uninvited houseguest and to find out if you are taking the case."

"Betty, I'm glad you called. I was going to call and tell you that you had Sarah's name correct and we haven't sensed her presence in our motorhome since we arrived back at the campground."

"That's all good news. I am glad to hear Sarah left your motorhome. It could get quite nerve wracking having a spirit traipsing around in those close quarters."

"Now that we know who she is and what she wants us to do she would still be welcome to stay. I kind of miss her and worry about her," Helen said.

"I'm sure that is your motherly instinct talking, Helen. Don't worry about Sarah. She will be just fine in her environment and I am sure she will be in occasional contact with you. It sounds like you and Hank are investigating her murder?"

"Yes, we are. We are still in the process of gathering background information. We'll keep you posted on our progress."

"OK, thanks, Helen. I'll let you get to it then."

"Thanks for calling, Betty. Bye."

Harry and Wilma were sitting outside their RV when Hank pulled into the space beside the Bounder. When they got out of the Honda Wilma waived and shouted, "Have you had any more raccoon problems, Helen?"

Helen waived back and said, "No more problems, Wilma. The raccoons are all quiet."

Hank carried Jim Rainey's case file into the Bounder and Helen followed with the guest registry printout.

Inside the Bounder, Hank removed the lid to Jim Rainey's case file. The file box contained hanging folders with tabs neatly printed and well organized.

Helen asked, "What is the best way to proceed with this?

"I think we both should read the entire file," Hank answered. "The crime scene photos might be a little tough for you to handle so you can skip those if you want." Hank thumbed through the hanging folders in the file box. "Aha, here is a folder on the questioning of the campers on the night of the murder. Why don't you start with this? As you read through the file put a check mark or make notes of anything significance alongside the corresponding names on the campground registration print-out. That way we'll have an idea who to talk with if they do indeed show up for this year's holiday. I'm going to start with the crime scene photos."

All told, only a few of the campers interviewed had provided information thought to be of significance. A Mrs. John Weaver saw one of the band's guitar players walking toward the lake with Sarah, presumably to watch the fireworks. The guitar player's name was Mike Beasley, whom Rainey later interviewed. The reported interview with Beasley read exactly as related by Rainey earlier in the day. Beasley had said he left Sarah sitting by the lake when he had to return to the bandstand for the last set.

Another camper couple with the last name of Riggs reported they saw Sarah sitting alone by the lake and when the band began to play they returned to their camper.

The case file's report on the discovery of the body was again exactly as Jim Rainey related to them earlier in the day. He had the girls name, Jennifer Higgins, correct who first noticed Sarah Payne's body. The boy who actually shook Sarah's body was named Brad Hildebrand. None of the teens interviewed saw or heard anything related to the murder as they were all up at the bandstand at the time.

After Helen marked up the campground registration sheets with the people named in the interviews she said, "I'm not coming up with anything different than what Jim told us earlier. How are you doing with the rest of the file?"

"Not much here either," Hank replied. I want to walk down to the crime scene to get the feel of it. We should be able to find the exact spot from the file photos. I scanned some copies to take along with us."

"All right, let's do it!" Helen replied

As they approached the lake Hank said, "According to the file, Sarah's body was found near the footbridge that crosses over a small feeder stream flowing into the lake."

"That looks like the bridge over there to the left," Helen said.

Hank studied the file photos as they neared the bridge, "Ok, according to the photos she was found on the other side of the bridge. Those two tall trees over there were in the background. The lake must have been at the photographer's back."

They crossed the bridge and lined themselves up with the two photographed trees. As they did, Helen glanced down at the ground and noticed the exposed top of what looked like a large embedded boulder. Pointing to it Helen said, "Is that the rock the police believe Sarah struck her head on?

"It looks very similar to the rock in the photo," Hank replied. "I'm surprised it is still exposed after eleven years."

A quick search around the area produced no other exposed rocks. Hank knelt down closer to the rock to better compare it to the picture. "I'm sure this is the same rock. It has the same shaped protuberance in the center. We must be standing in the exact spot where Sarah's body had lain."

Helen shivered from a sudden chill on the back of her neck and quickly turned to look behind her. "Hank, did you just feel a sudden chill. It was like the ones we felt in the Bounder?"

"No, I didn't feel it," Hank responded.

"I believe Sarah was just here to let us know we found the right spot. The poor girl has never left."

"Maybe you're right. You do seem to be sensitive in that area. Don't forget, you thought you saw Elvis when we visited Graceland a couple of years ago."

"Yes, and I felt the same type of chill when that happened," Helen said as she turned and looked out over the lake. "Hank, this isn't a very large lake. Mrs. Hartman said the fireworks display was set off from the opposite bank over there. That's only a couple hundred feet away."

"What are you thinking?" Hank asked.

"Well, Sarah's death occurred after the fireworks and while the band was playing its last set. It could be that the fireworks people were over there just across the lake cleaning up when the crime occurred. I don't recall from the file that anyone from the crew was interviewed."

"Hmm, great thinking," Hank replied. "We'll have to ask Jim Rainey about that. Well, I think we're done here. Let's head back to the Bounder."

Harry and Wilma Schultz were sitting on their patio when Hank and Helen walked by on the way to their campsite. "Were you two out looking for raccoons?" Wilma asked with a chuckle.

"No, just a quiet walk down by the lake," Helen replied.

"Well, the scuttlebutt around the campground is that you two are looking into the death of the girl that happened some time ago," Wilma added.

"Wow, news sure travels fast around here," Helen replied.

"They always say that news travels fast in a small town. Found any clues yet?" Wilma inquired.

"No Wilma, not yet, it is still very early in our investigation."

"Well, good luck. If you need some ears to the ground, let us know."

"Will do, Wilma," Helen light heartily replied.

When Hank and Helen retreated to the inside the bounder, Helen asked, "What's on the agenda for tomorrow?"

"Not much we can do until all of the campers arrive," Hank replied. "We have to get the copies of this year's campground registration before we can start asking questions. What do you suggest?"

"Well, we can ask Mrs. Hartman about the fireworks company. She should have their contact information. And we could stop by the library to see if Mrs. Fritch the librarian is back in town. What Wilma said about news traveling fast in a small town is true. Maybe Mrs. Fritch remembers the old scuttlebutt about the murder."

On Thursday morning Hank volunteered to make breakfast sandwiches with eggs, bacon, and cheese on toasted English muffins, which he created one at a time in a small one egg wonder frying pan. Helen always marveled how Hank could produce such a delicious meal with only one small pan to clean afterward.

With breakfast completed, they walked to Mrs. Hartman's house at the entrance to the campground. Her vintage blue Chrysler was parked in the driveway and Mrs. Hartman was sitting on her front porch nursing a mug of coffee.

"Good morning, Mrs. Hartman," Helen said as they approached the porch. "Could you spare us a few minutes of your time this morning?"

"Sure, come on up and sit down," Mrs. Hartman replied. "I'd offer you some coffee but I think my grandson Eddie just emptied the pot."

"That's ok, we've had plenty already," Helen replied. "We'd like to ask you a few more questions about the night Sarah Payne was murdered."

"Well ok, what would you like to know?"

"We would like information on the company that put on the fireworks display that night. I understand they set up just across the lake from the murder scene," Helen said.

"It is a small company from down in Thomasville and yes they set up the display just across the lake," Mrs. Hartman replied.

"How many persons were there from the fireworks company," Hank asked.

"Only two, Mr. Higgin's the company owner and one assistant who back then was his teenaged nephew."

"Would you still have contact information for Mr. Higgin's company?" Helen inquired.

"Yes, I do. But if you want to question Mr. Higgins he should be arriving here on Friday afternoon."

"Oh, you hired the same company you had back in two thousand and three?"

"Yes, Mr. Higgins has been providing his services for the last fourteen years. He does it more or less as a hobby."

"Would you do us a favor and inform Mr. Higgin's we would like to talk to him when he arrives?" Hank asked.

"I sure will," Mrs. Hartman replied. "Is there anything else Mr. Moran?"

"That's all for now, Mrs. Hartman. Thanks for your help."

Chapter 6

As Hank and Helen were driving to the Thomas County Library Helen asked, "When do you think we should contact Sarah's parents about our investigation?"

"If we are successful in finding Sarah's murderer I am sure the Sheriff's office would want to contact them," Hank replied. "If you remember, they were sitting out in front of their motorhome and oblivious to what had happened to their daughter until Sheriff Rainey informed them. And according to Rainey's case file, they provided nothing useful to the investigation. So I see no immediate need to contact them."

"Wouldn't they want to know that Sarah's spirit is still present at the campground?" Helen asked.

"I think the real question is; Would Sarah want them to know?" Hank replied.

"You have a point there, I would think not," Helen replied.

Upon entering the library, they spotted a late middle-aged woman wearing a polka dot dress, reading glasses, and gray hair in a bun, sitting at the librarian's desk and approached her.

"Good morning ma'am, are you Mrs. Fritch?" Helen asked.

"Yes, I am. How can I help you?" Mrs. Fritch replied looking over the top of her reading glasses.

"My name is Helen Moran and this is my Husband Hank. We're from the Moran Investigations Agency and we are investigating a murder that occurred at the Ochlocknee Campground back in two thousand three."

"Oh, you must be referring to the Payne girl's murder. Do you want to peruse the newspaper archives?" Mrs. Fritch asked.

"No, we went through the papers yesterday and Mrs. Weston was very helpful," Helen replied.

"Then how else can I help you?" Mrs. Fritch inquired.

"We know how news and rumors travel fast in a small town so we're hoping you could perhaps provide some information and background that would not appear in the police file."

"I see. I'm not one to pass on rumors or idle gossip but I did hear a few things after the murder," Mrs. Fritch replied.

"Would you like to share them with us?" Helen asked.

Mrs. Fritch began, "Well, there was lots of speculation as to who the murderer might be. Some people thought it must have been someone from the fireworks company as they would have been in the crime scene area at the time. Some people thought it was a serial killer who traveled around to different campgrounds killing young girls. Hicks, the newspaper reporter checked out the serial killer idea with the FBI and they came up blank."

"Did you suspect anyone at the time," Helen asked.

"I had some ideas, but nothing really specific," Mrs. Fritch replied. "They ruled out members of the rock band because they were performing at the time, but the band had two roadies who would have had some free time to do it. Then there were over eighty sites full of campers. Most were small decent families, but I would have looked for a lone male camper or a dysfunctional family with a troubled teenager. I would like to be of more help in your investigation but I think I told you everything I know."

"Well, you've been a great help, Mrs. Fritch," Helen said. "We'll be sure to check out some of your ideas."

Once outside the library Helen said, "I am sure news of our little visit to the library will be all over town in twenty minutes."

"I was thinking more like fifteen," Hank replied. "I was planning to call Agent Emory up at the Tennessee FBI field office to check on the serial killer idea. Even though reporter Hicks contacted the FBI back in two thousand three I still might give him a call."

"Do you think they might have missed something back then?" Helen asked.

"No, but I was thinking about how the Leviticus murders progressed two years ago. The FBI didn't put two and two together until after the third killing. And who knows, maybe Sarah's murder was just the beginning of a series."

Hank had recently purchased a new smartphone and had all his contacts transferred to it from his old phone. When he and Helen returned to the Honda Hank asked Helen to drive so he could make a call.

Hank found Agent Chris Emory in his contact list and tapped the phone icon next to his name. Emory answered on the fourth ring. "Hello, Hank. How are you and Helen?"

"Hello, Chris. We're doin' fine. I'm impressed that you still have my number in your caller I.D.," Hank replied.

"Well, you never know when I would need some expert advice on a case."

"Well Chris, expert advice is what I'm calling you about. We're looking into a cold case down in Georgia and we're hoping you could check something on the national crime database."

"You're working a case? Are you back on the force?"

"No, Chris. Helen and I have opened a private investigation firm and are doing quite well with it. We were on our way to Charleston for a little vacation break and got involved with a cold case at a campground near Thomasville, Georgia."

"I see, what is the nature of the case?"

"A teenage girl was raped and strangled to death at the campground back in two thousand three. I was hoping you could check to see if there were any similar cases at southeastern campgrounds since that time."

"Hank, do you think you might have come across another serial situation."

"Chris, I just want to eliminate that possibility to narrow our scope on the case. Right now we don't have much to go on and eliminating that possibility would perhaps help point us to a suspect from the local area."

"I see. I am sure there are loads of rape and strangulation cases, but if I narrow the search to the crimes being committed at campgrounds and in addition in the southeastern states it would make it a lot more manageable."

"That should work just fine, Chris. We'd appreciate any help we could get."

"Ok, Hank. I'll get right on it. By the way, I guess you heard that our preacher friend got life without parole for the Leviticus murders."

"Yes I did, Chris. I guess now he has a captive congregation to preach to."

"You're right; it would be interesting to see if his brand of religion goes over well in a state pen."

"If anything, I am sure he will keep the other inmates entertained," Hank replied.

"Probably in more ways than one if you catch my drift, Hank."

"It couldn't happen to a nicer guy Chris."

"Ok Hank, it was good to hear from you again and I'll get back with you on the search."

"Thanks, Chris; I'll be waiting for your call."

Upon disconnecting the call to agent Emory, Hank immediately tapped the call icon behind Jim Rainey's name in his directory and made sure the speaker was on. The ex-sheriff answered on the third ring. "Good morning Hank, do you have an update on the case?"

"Good morning Jim. We looked through your case file and found nothing that really stood out except Helen noticed there was no mention of an interview with the fireworks vendor."

"That is correct Hank. Mr. Higgins and his nephew stopped by Mrs. Hartman's house on their way out to pick up a check for payment for the fireworks display. That was right before the band started its last set. They were due back in the morning to do a final cleanup and to retrieve what equipment they had left behind."

"So, then it is safe to assume they were not present at the campground when the murder occurred," Hank replied.

"That is correct Hank. Mrs. Hartman recalled watching their truck leave through the campground entrance and a few minutes later the band started playing," Rainey added.

"Jim, How far away is Mr. Higgins business from the campground and where does his nephew live?" Hank inquired.

"Higgins is from just north of Thomasville and his nephew lives just west of the campground on Lockerman Road," Rainey replied.

"So then Higgins probably dropped off his nephew before heading home to Thomasville. Just how far is it from the campground to his nephew's house?" Hank inquired further.

"Damn it, just a few hundred yards through the woods behind the lake. I'm afraid that is something I neglected to cover in my investigation, Hank."

"What is the nephew's name and does he still live at the same place?" Hank asked.

"His name is Jake, his brother's boy, same last name. I don't know his present whereabouts," Hank.

"Ok, Jim, we'll check on him," Hank replied.

"Sheriff Rainey, this is Helen, I noticed the girl who first discovered Sarah Payne's body, has the last name of Higgins, the same as the fireworks company, would they happen to be related also?"

"Good question Helen. I see you astutely picked up on that little coincidence. It turned out that Jennifer Higgins is not related in any way to Mr. Higgins who owns the fireworks company."

"Thank you, Sheriff," Helen replied.

"Jim, tomorrow we will be questioning campers who were present at the campground when Sarah Payne was murdered. There are quite a few who will be at this year's event. Would you be interested in sitting in and aiding with the interviews?" Hank asked.

"You couldn't keep me away," Rainey replied. "What time do you want me there?"

"Would around ten tomorrow morning be ok?"

"Sounds good Hank, I'll be there."

"Oh Jim, one more thing, do you happen to know if Beasley the guitar player still lives in the area?"

"Yes, he does. In fact, he has a local real estate company. You should find him on Google."

"Thanks, Jim, see you in the morning," Hank said as he ended the call.

After their conversation with Jim Rainey, Helen said, "Well Hank that was interesting about Higgin's nephew. I can't imagine that a teenager could resist the lure of a rock band with only a few minutes' walk through the woods."

"We'll ask Mr. Higgins about his nephew tomorrow afternoon. In the meantime, why don't we try to track down Mr. Beasley at his real estate company and have a chat with him?" Hank replied.

Helen googled Beasley real estate and found a listing for a Beasley Real Estate Company on North Broad Street. She entered the address into her GPS app and realized Beasley's office was only down the street and around the corner a few city blocks from the library. They pulled into the real estate office's small parking lot five minutes later.

Beasley's real estate office was a small one-story building with wooden steps and a small covered porch leading to the front door. The whole building including the porch was in desperate need of a paint job which did not go unnoticed by Hank as he chuckled and said, "It looks like sales must be slow. The condition of the building doesn't give a good first impression if you are trying to sell real estate."

Chapter 7

The office Hank and Helen entered was small with no reception area and only two desks with a couple of chairs in front of them. One desk was empty and the other was occupied by a blond-haired man in his late twenties dressed in a blue polo shirt and jeans. On the wall next to the man was an enlarged photo of a rock band called the Bees.

The man looked up with a growing smile thinking he might have a couple interested in buying a house. "Good morning folks. I'm Mike Beasley, how can I help you?"

"Good morning Mr. Beasley, I am Hank Moran and this is my wife Helen. We are from the Moran Investigations Agency and are here looking into the murder of Sarah Payne that occurred back in two thousand and three. We would like to take a few minutes of your time and ask you a few questions."

The smile on Beasley's face quickly faded when he realized the couple in front of him wasn't interested in real estate. "Wow, that was some time ago. I haven't thought about that girl's murder in years. You say you're from an agency and not the police?"

"That's right," Hank answered. "We are investigating at the request of a client."

"Okaaay, why do you want to question me?" Beasley inquired.

"We understand your rock band provided the music for the night the murder occurred and that you struck up a relationship with the deceased. What can you tell us about that?" Hank asked.

Beasley with a perplexed expression on his face replied, "Ok, I really don't know where to start."

"Just start from the time you and the band arrived at the campground and relate to the best of your knowledge the entire evening's events," Hank replied.

Beasley sat back and composed himself a brief moment and then started, "Best as I can remember we arrived at the campground around seven to set up. That took about a good half an hour and then did a final test and tune-up of our instruments. We had about ten minutes to take a break before we had to start the gig, so we mingled a little with the kids that were starting to gather around. I noticed a good looking girl who looked about eighteen, approached her and struck up a conversation. I invited her to stick around after the set so we could watch the fireworks together, she said ok and that she would enjoy the company."

"Who was the girl you talked to?" Hank asked.

"It was Sarah Payne," Beasley replied.

"Did she stay and watch the band during the whole set?" Helen asked.

"I was too busy playing to notice the whole time but she was there for the last song. After we were finished playing Sarah and I got a coke from the bands cooler and then we walked down to the lake together to watch the fireworks."

"What did you talk about during that time?" Helen asked.

"Well we couldn't talk about much because of all the noise from the fireworks, but I gathered she was upset about her choice of college in the fall," Beasley replied.

"What happened after the fireworks were finished," Hank asked.

"I offered to walk her back to the bandstand to listen to the last set but she said she wanted to sit by the lake and think a while about her choice of college, so I said I would look for her after the last set. That was the last I saw her alive," Beasley stated.

"Did you leave the stage at all during the last set?" Hank asked.

"Are you kidding? How could I leave in the middle of a set? I was the lead guitarist and did backup vocals. No way could I leave the stage."

"How about the other band members, were they on stage the whole time?" Helen asked.

"Yes they were, there were only four of us in the band and there was no way that we could play without one of us."

"Ok, how about your roadies. How many did you have and were they required to be present during your performance?" Hank inquired.

"Why are you people so interested in the band when there was a whole campground full of people that could have done it?" Beasley asked with a touch of anger.

"Mr. Beasley, so far it seems that you were the last person to converse with Sarah Payne before she was brutally murdered. So that is why we are questioning you. Did you mention to your roadies that Miss Payne was sitting alone down by the lake?" Hank inquired.

"Mr. Moran, we only had two roadies and one of them was needed to monitor and adjust the sound system for different songs. The other one just hung around the stage. I might have said something in passing about meeting Sarah but I don't recall saying anything about her sitting alone down by the lake."

"Ok, what is the name of the roadie that just hung around the stage," Hank asked.

"His name is Charlie Hewitt," Beasley replied.

"Does Mr. Hewitt still live in the area and if he does do you know his address and phone number," Hank asked.

"Charlie lives up on East Walcott and I have his number right here." Beasley gave Hewitt's address and phone number to Hank.

"He's probably working right now. He works for the county road crew," Beasley further stated.

"Mr. Beasley, do you still have your rock band together?" Helen asked.

"No Mrs. Moran, as it turned out the gig at the campground was our last one. Three of us headed off to different colleges a month and a half later."

"I am curious about the name of the band. Was it a take on your last name?" Helen further asked.

"You guessed it, Mrs. Moran. The name "b e A s" would have looked a little odd so we just called our band the "Bees"."

"Mr. Beasley, would you mind if I snapped a photo of your band pic for our records," Helen asked.

Beasley smiled and said, "I guess it would be ok. Help yourself. By the way, that picture was taken just before we started playing that night"

Helen stood and used her cell phone to snap the picture and then nodded to Hank, meaning that she had no further questions.

Hank also rose and said, "Ok Mr. Beasley that is all of the questions for now. Thank you for your time and for talking to us. Here is my card. Please call us if you think of anything at all that could help us in solving Miss Payne's murder."

"I will do that, Mr. and Mrs. Moran. You wouldn't by any chance be interested in any real estate in the area would you," Beasley inquired.

"I'm afraid not," Hank replied as they headed for the door.

Back in the Honda Hank stated, "Well that was a waste of time except for the name of the band's roadie."

"I had a feeling that I should take that picture of Beasley's band. I think it may come in handy," Helen said as she opened the pic on her cell phone. The pic centered on the four playing members of the band with two other guys, one standing at each end of the group. Helen assumed the guys at the ends were the roadies. There were numerous other teenagers around the periphery.

Helen handed the phone to Hank so he could see the photo. "Not a bad looking group for a rock band except for the guy on the end with the shaved head. I wonder which one is Charlie Hewitt," Hank said.

Hank handed the phone back to Helen and she entered Hewitt's number onto her phones contacts list. "Shall I give Mr. Hewitt a call?" Helen asked.

"I guess there's no time like the present," Hank replied. "We have some time before I want to get back to the campground. I want to take another look through Sheriff Rainey's case file before I return it to him tomorrow."

Helen punched in Hewitt's number and he answered on the fourth ring. He must have noticed the call was coming from an unfamiliar number. "This is Charlie, who's calling and what do you want?" was his brusque answer.

"Hello Mr. Hewitt, I am Helen Moran from Moran Investigations. Would you have some time to meet with my partner and me today? We have a few questions about the Sarah Payne murder which happened ten years ago at the Ochlocknee Campground."

"Say what? Is this some crank call about my truck warranty or something," Hewitt loudly replied.

"No, this is Helen Moran from Moran Investigations. We are investigating" . . .

"I can't hear you. There's too much machinery noise out here. Sorry," Hewitt interrupted before he abruptly cut off the call.

Hank heard the call as Helen had it on the speaker.

"Hmm, I didn't hear any machinery noise in the background. Do you think he might have been avoiding the call because you mentioned Sarah Payne," Hank asked.

"The same thought crossed my mind," Helen replied. "But for now I'm willing to give him the benefit of the doubt. We might not have heard the machinery because of the Honda idling with the A.C. on, "We'll have to try to catch him later at his home."

"You may be right," Hank replied as he put the Honda in gear.

Before Hank could back out of the parking lot his cell phone rang and he saw it was a call from Agent Emory. Shifting back to park, he answered the call and put it on the speaker, "Hello Chris, what's up."

"Hello Hank, I searched our database as I mentioned before and came up with three rape cases with only one murder involved at southern campgrounds during the last eleven years. The one rape-murder happens to be the case you are involved in. In the other two rape cases, the victims knew the perps and only one was prosecuted with charges being dropped because of a debatable consent issue."

"Did either of the other two cases happen in this area?" Hank inquired.

"Afraid not Hank, one was in Florida and the other in South Carolina."

"Well Chris, I guess I can rule out a serial situation. Thanks for getting back so quickly."

"I am glad to help anytime Hank and good luck in your case."

"Thanks again Chris, bye."

"Well partner, it looks like we'll be looking for someone local or some fellow camper," Hank said when the call from Emory was ended.

"I guess we always thought that was the case," Helen replied. "The serial killer option was always an extreme longshot."

"You're right," Hank replied. "At least we don't have to worry about that any longer."

Chapter 8

"I've got an idea! What if I call the county road department and find out when Hewitt's shift ends," Helen suggested.

"Good idea," Hank replied. Maybe you can also find out where in the county he's working. We might be able to talk with him on the job instead of waiting for him to get home."

Helen googled the Thomas County Public Works office and gave them a call. She found out that normally the road crews shift ends at three thirty. After some persistence, she also found out that Charlie Hewitt was scheduled to work with the mower crew on Coffee Road. Helen used her map app to find Coffee Road. "Alright, if we go northeast on Rt. 122 for about eight miles we will come to the intersection of Coffee Road on the right," Helen said.

"Ok let's go," Hank replied. "Maybe we can catch him on his lunch break. Point me in the direction of 122."

Twenty minutes later Hank made the right turn onto Coffee Road, motored about two miles and pulled behind a white Thomas County Public Works pickup truck. He exited the Honda, walked up to the truck and tapped on the driver's side window. The man sitting in the driver's seat jerked his head up, looked at Hank and lowered the window.

"Can I help you, buddy," the man said.

"We're looking for Charlie Hewitt. We called the head-quarters and they said he was working out here today," Hank replied.

The man, seemingly unconcerned, replied that Hewitt was down the road about a quarter mile sitting under the shade tree on the left.

Hank thanked the man, got back into the Honda, and drove the quarter mile down the road. There were two men relaxing in the shade on the left. Hank parked on the right side berm, exited the Honda, and approached the men.

"Sorry to interrupt your break gentlemen but we need to talk with Charlie Hewitt for a few minutes."

The man on the right wearing a soiled roads division t-shirt and ball cap replied, "I'm Charlie, what do you want?"

Hank noticed the ball cap fit low to Hewitt's ears most likely because he had a shaved head. "I'm Hank Moran from The Moran Investigations Agency," I need to talk with you a few minutes about the Sarah Payne murder that happened over at the Ochlocknee campground eleven years ago. We'd appreciate it if you could spare a few minutes of your time."

"You want to talk now?" Hewitt replied.

"Yes, we'd like to talk now. We can sit in the Honda over there. It's air-conditioned," Hank replied.

"Well ok, you got me curious. I completely forgot about that little incident," Hewitt replied as he rose to follow Hank to the Honda.

Helen moved to the back seat to make more room for Hewitt. When all were seated Hank introduced Helen as his agency partner.

"Okay, what do you want to talk about?" asked Hewitt.

"Mr. Hewitt, as I stated earlier, we are investigating the rape and murder of Sarah Payne at the Ochlocknee Campground in two thousand three. We talked with Mike Beasley earlier today and he told us you were the roadie for the band and that you had some free time during the band's performance. We would like you to think back and try to remember if you saw anything or anybody that looked suspicious during the band's last set."

"Gee, that was a long time ago. The police questioned me at the time and I told them back then I hadn't seen anything that would be of use," Hewitt replied.

"We know that Mike Beasley had struck up a casual relationship with Sarah that evening. He stated he watched the fireworks with her down at the lake and then left her there to play the band's last set. Do you remember that?" queried Hank.

"Yeah, I remember that," stated Hewitt. "Mike was very interested in the girl and wanted to hook up with her after the set. Before they started playing he asked me to walk down to the lake to ask her to come up to the stage area when she was done with her thinking. I walked down there and found her and told her about Mike's request and she said she would. I found out later from Mike that she was thinking about her choice of college."

Hank glanced back at Helen with raised eyebrows and asked Hewitt, "How long did you stay at the lake with Sarah?"

"It was only a minute or two, and then I walked back up to the stage in case I was needed to replace a broken guitar string or whatever."

"I see," Hank said. I don't remember reading about your contact with Sarah in the police files. Did you mention that when they questioned you?"

"No, I was afraid to mention it at the time thinking I would be a suspect because the murder happened during the last set."

"Hmm, would Mike Beasley verify that you came right back to the stage area," Hank asked.

"I am sure he would because right between the second and third songs he asked me to check the tuning on his spare Stratocaster guitar," Hewitt replied. "The other band members would verify it also."

"Now, when you were down at the lake talking with Sarah did you see anyone lurking around or anyone who looked suspicious?" Hank inquired.

"No, not really. The only person I saw nearby was Mrs. Hartman's grandson Eddie just across the lake where they set off the fireworks."

"What did it look like Eddie was doing over there?" Hank asked with a hint of excitement.

"It looked like he was just fooling around with the spent rocket casings, and he was still there when I left," Hewitt replied.

Hank turned back to Helen and asked, "Helen, do you have anything you'd like to ask Mr. Hewitt?"

"Just one thing," Helen said as she pulled up the band's picture on her phone and showed it to Hewitt. "Is that you on the far left side of the picture?"

"Yeah, that's me alright, me and my bald head. I developed a small cancerous brain tumor when I was sixteen and lost my hair during chemo. For some crazy idea, I liked the look and shaved my head ever since. Thankfully the doc declared I was in complete remission two years later right before that picture was taken."

"Congratulations on your victory!" Helen replied.

"Thank you, Mrs. Moran," Hewitt replied.

Ok, Mr. Hewitt, that's all the questions we have for now," Hank said. "Here is my card. Please call us if anything else comes to mind about that evening. Thank you for your time. We really appreciate it."

"Anytime," Hewitt said as he exited the Honda.

"Finally, we have something that might help!" Helen said as she reentered the front seat. "That little bit of information about Eddie being on the other side of the lake is very interesting indeed. And do you remember how he reacted the other day when we mentioned our investigation into Sarah Payne's death"

"I do remember. He actually looked scared. He could be a possible witness," Hank said. "Let's head back to the campground. I want to review Sheriff Rainey's case file again and then give him a call. By the way, how did you feel about Charlie Hewitt? Do you think he was being truthful?"

"He seemed to be telling the truth," Helen replied. "I'd feel better about him if we could verify exactly when he was attending to things during the band's last performance."

"I agree," Hank replied. "I recall that in the case file a deputy did interview him. But if he neglected to mention the fact he went down to the lake to talk to Sarah they would not have questioned his whereabouts. Let's give Mike Beasley a call. Either Beasley lied to us about not mentioning to his roadie about Sarah sitting down by the lake or he has a very bad memory."

Helen called Mike Beasley's number and put it on the speaker. After a few rings, Beasley answered, "Beasley Real Estate how can I be of service?"

"Mr. Beasley this is Hank Moran, I have a few more questions to ask about the Sarah Payne case."

"Ok Detective Moran, what do you need?"

"We just got finished talking with Charlie Hewitt and we need to verify a statement of his. He claims that before your band started the last set you asked him to go down to the lake to invite Sarah Payne back to the stage. Do you recall making that request?"

After a slight pause Beasley apologetically replied, "Yes, Mr. Moran, I did ask him to do that. I'm sorry I left it out. I didn't mention it before because I thought it might get Charlie in trouble."

"I see, do you recall how long he was gone?" Hank asked.

"Boy, let me think a minute. . . . I don't think he was gone very long because I remember him checking the tuning on my Stratocaster and if I remember correctly I needed that guitar for our second or third song. So he could not have been gone longer than about fifteen minutes."

"Are you sure of that Mr. Beasley? You're not leaving anything else out?"

"I'm as sure as can be trying to remember details about something that happened ten or eleven years ago," Beasley replied.

"Ok Mr. Beasley, that helps a great deal. Thank you for your time and good luck with your business."

"Thank you, detective, I need all the luck I can muster these days. If you need anything else I'll try to help the best I can."

After ending the call Hank said, "Well that more or less clears Charlie Hewitt, assuming, of course, Hewitt didn't hurry up and call Beasley in the last five minutes to tell him to back up his statement to us."

"Hank, I'll bet he didn't do it because Beasley's phone would have been busy when you called. Old buddies would have talked longer than a minute or two. And a better reason is, he is still sitting across the road and I didn't see him make a call."

Hank just looked at Helen and smiled, "Let's head back to the campground partner."

As they drove into the campground entrance Helen told Hank to stop in front of the office so she could check with Ruth on the availability of the camper's registration copies. As Helen entered the office she noticed Eddie sitting in a chair in the lounge area. When Eddie noticed Helen he abruptly arose and left by the rear door.

After watching Eddie leave Helen turned to Ruth and asked, "Hi Ruth. How's it going with the incoming camper registrations?"

"Almost everyone is here for the weekend," Ruth replied. A few more will be checking in before evening and a few tomorrow before noon. I can make you a copy of what we have so far if you think it would be helpful."

Helen thought a second and replied, "Yes I would like that and would it be possible to get a copy of the reservations for the campers still due to check in? That way we won't have to bother you again."

"Sure Mrs. Moran, I can do that if you want to wait a minute."

"That would be great. Thanks, Ruth."

A few minutes later Helen was back in the Honda with the needed copies. "I got all the copies we need for comparison of this year's campers to two thousand and three," Helen said. "And when I entered the office, Eddie was sitting in the lounge area. When he saw me he hurried and got up and left by the rear door."

"There is definitely something going on with Eddie. I am sure he knows something that's making him fearful of interacting with us," Hank replied. "We'll have to talk with Eddie's grandmother about his actions and the right way to approach the subject with him. I have no experience in questioning a person with the Down syndrome."

Chapter 9

Harry and Wilma were sitting out on their patio and waved when Hank pulled up and parked by the Bounder. Hank and Helen waved back as they entered their motorhome.

"The first thing I want to do is call Jim Rainey and tell him about Hewitt's statement concerning Eddie," Hank said as he punched Rainey's entry on his list of phone contacts.

Rainey's phone chimed and seeing it was Hank calling he tapped on the answer icon, "Good afternoon Hank, what's happening?"

"Good afternoon Jim, I want to pass some information on to you that we heard from one of the band's roadies, Charles Hewitt. He stated Beasley sent him down to the lake to give a message to Sarah Payne right before the band's last set. He was to tell Sarah Payne to come back to the stage when she was done thinking about college. While Hewitt was down at the lake he claims he saw Mrs. Hartman's grandson Eddie across the lake fooling with spent firework's rocket casings. Did any of this come up during your investigation?"

"Damn, this is all news to me," Rainey replied. "Does this mean Hewitt is a suspect?"

"I'm afraid not, Jim. We verified that he was down at the lake only a short time before he went back up to the band. But Eddie could be a possible witness to the crime."

"Good heavens, this never came up in our investigation, Hank. You might just be getting somewhere in this case."

"Eddie acted strangely and quickly left the campground office when we mentioned to him we were investigating Sarah's murder, and on another occasion, he quickly left the office as soon as Mrs. Moran entered. I have a strong feeling he knows something that has him scared to associate with us. I would appreciate it if you could sit down with us and Mrs. Hartman tomorrow morning to discuss the best way to question Eddie. We haven't mentioned this to Mrs. Hartman as yet."

"I would be glad to, Hank. I can see where it would be a delicate situation and I think Mrs. Hartman would feel more comfortable if I was there."

"Ok, thanks, Jim. I'll call Mrs. Hartman right away and try to set up the meeting. I assume you are still coming at ten tomorrow morning to start questioning the campers. If so, we can start with our talk with Mrs. Hartman."

"Sounds good Hank, I'll surely be there."

When the call to Rainey ended Helen asked, "Do you think we should call Mrs. Hartman or walk over there?" She might be sitting out on her front porch and I'd hate to make her get up to answer the phone."

"I guess you're right," Hank replied. "We should try to make this as less stressful for her as possible."

"You must be psychic. She is sitting out on her front porch." Hank said as they neared Mrs. Hartman's house.

"I'm not psychic, big guy. Sitting on front porches is what retired people do," Helen replied.

"Huh, I'm retired, how come I don't sit more on our front porch," Hank responded.

"Because you are not retired, Hank. Running our agency is approaching full-time work status."

"Do you think we should cut back some?" Hank asked.

"That was what this trip to Charleston was supposed to be for, but it didn't work out that way," Helen replied with a chuckle.

"Good afternoon Mrs. Hartman," Helen said as they stopped in front of Mrs. Hartman's front porch.

"Well, good afternoon detectives, to what do I owe this visit?"

"We need to talk to you about some information we uncovered during our investigation. It concerns your grandson Eddie," Hank replied.

"My grandson? Come up and sit down and tell me what this is all about."

Hank and Helen stepped up onto the porch and sat down in two chairs facing Mrs. Hartman. Hank then proceeded to give the reason for their visit. "Mrs. Hartman, we interviewed a man named Charles Hewitt who claims he saw Eddie on the far side of the lake picking up spent firework rocket casings just prior to the time of Sarah Payne's murder. Mr. Hewitt, who at that time was one of the band's roadies, spoke briefly to Miss Payne and left to go back to the stage where the band was playing. We believe Eddie may have been a witness to the crime."

"I thought you were going to say that Eddie is a suspect," Mrs. Hartman indignantly replied.

"No, we don't think that at all, Mrs. Hartman," Helen replied. "However it seems Eddie deliberately tries to avoid us after he learned we are investigating the murder. I think he is fearful of associating with us."

"Well, Eddie being a witness may explain why he acted so strange that whole weekend until he went home Sunday evening."

"In what way did he act strange, Mrs. Hartman?" Helen asked.

"After it happened he seemed very jittery and didn't leave my side. I thought it may have been due to just the trauma of something like that happening at the campground. We were all upset about it and I figured he may have just picked up on my fears."

"Mrs. Hartman, Jim Rainey is coming here at ten tomorrow morning to aid in questioning some campers who were here at the time. Would it be possible for all of us to sit down and question Eddie about that night?" Hank asked.

"Yes, I think we have to if it could help solve the crime," Mrs. Hartman replied. "I won't mention anything to him until we are all gathered. I don't want him to worry any longer than necessary."

"Thank you for your cooperation, Mrs. Hartman. We'll be here as soon as Jim Rainey arrives," Hank said.

"I'm glad Jim is involved. He's been fretting about this case ever since he retired," Mrs. Hartman said. "He must be excited about a possible break."

"Yes he is, Mrs. Hartman, we'll see you and Eddie at ten tomorrow morning," Hank replied.

Hank and Helen walked back to their motorhome after making arrangements with Mrs. Hartman. It was impossible to avoid Harry and Wilma Schultz who were sitting out on their patio watching the arriving campers.

"Good afternoon folks! How are things going in your investigation?" Wilma inquired.

"Hi Wilma and Harry, as of now we have ninety-three suspects on our list. If you folks have an airtight alibi we can reduce the list to ninety-one," Helen jokingly replied.

"We arrived here five years after the crime took place and I don't think time travel is proven yet. So I think we have a pretty good alibi," Harry laughingly replied.

"Well Hank, I think we can cross the Schultz's off our list," Helen joked. "You folks have a nice day, we have to go and question the other ninety-one suspects."

"Well, we wish you good luck," Wilma replied.

Late that afternoon Hank searched back through Jim Rainey's case file, making a list of the twelve campers previously interviewed on the night of the murder. Only three of the twelve mentioned in the file had semi-useful input. One couple saw Beasley sitting with Sarah Payne during the fireworks. Another couple saw Sarah Payne sitting alone shortly after the fireworks ended. And in another entry that piqued Hank's interest, a couple sitting out in front of their camping trailer stated they saw Eddie running fairly fast towards his grandmother's house shortly before the band quit playing the last set. Apparently the other seventy some campers had contributed nothing of importance to merit entry into the case file.

Helen spent an hour comparing the two thousand and three camper registration list with the present years and found a total of seventeen present registrants who were on site ten years ago. She made a separate list of the seventeen and noted the site number behind each name. Helen printed out a copy of the list and handed it to Hank.

Hank compared Helen's list of seventeen campers to his list of campers interviewed by the sheriff's department ten years ago and found only five, which included the three with semi-useful input, have returned to the campground this year.

"Well we have seventeen returning campers and only five of them were mentioned in the case file as being interviewed back then," Hank stated. "I hate to be a pessimist but it doesn't look very promising for our interviews tomorrow."

"Hank, you are forgetting Eddie's possible input in the morning. My intuition tells me we might be dealing with an entirely different situation during those interviews tomorrow. And all of this research made me hungry. Let's go into town and have a good sit down meal this evening."

"You don't have to mention it twice!" Hank said. "I'm really steak hungry. You head into the shower first but don't use all of the hot water."

"You're the one who always uses up the hot water," Helen retorted as she hurried towards the rear of the motorhome. "I heard that the Chophouse is the best place for steaks. See if you can find their number and make reservations," she added before entering the rear bath.

One hour later they were sitting in The Chophouse Restaurant sharing an appetizer of gulf shrimp cakes topped with a creole mustard sauce while waiting on their entrees. Helen had ordered the petite filet mignon and Hank opted for the dry aged ribeye. While enjoying dinner their conversation about the Sarah Payne investigation was overheard by a couple sitting at the next table. As the couple was leaving they stopped at Hank and Helen's table.

The man was fifty-something in age and wore a white Fleetwood Bounder t-shirt, navy blue shorts and white sneakers with socks. The woman was similarly attired except she opted for white sandals sans socks.

"Excuse us, folks, my name is Bill Weaver and this is my wife Rachael. We overheard you discussing the murder of the girl that took place here about ten years ago. We were camping here at the time. Are you folks from the agency that is here doing the investigation?"

"Yes we are Mr. Weaver, I am Hank Moran and this is my wife Helen," Hank said as he stood and shook hands with the couple. "I remember reading in the sheriff's case file that both of you were interviewed the night of the murder."

"Yes we were, but we really didn't contribute much in the way of information. We both saw a guy, who turned out to be the guitar player, walking with the girl down towards the lake before the fireworks and afterward walk back up by our site towards the band's stage."

"That gentleman was Mike Beasley, the lead guitarist, and is not a suspect in the case," Hank stated and then decided to change the subject. "By the way that is an interesting shirt you have on. Do you folks own a Bounder?

"Yes, we do the blue and white one in site forty-nine. This is our maiden voyage in it. We just traded in our travel trailer for something bigger."

"What floor plan is it?" Hank asked.

"It's a thirty-five K," Weaver replied.

"Our Bounder is a couple of years old with the same floor plan. It's the black and gold one in site twenty-two," Hank said. "We'll look for yours tomorrow when we re-interview a few of the campers that were here ten years ago."

"Ok, stop on by and we'll show you around our new rig," Weaver said.

"Will do, and have a nice evening," Hank replied.

"You folks have a nice evening also," Carl Weaver said as they turned and headed for the door.

"They seemed like a nice couple," Helen said. "Are we going to reinterview them tomorrow?"

"I think we should drop by. We might have a few different questions to ask after we talk with Eddie tomorrow morning," Hank replied. "By the way what's for dessert?"

"Cheesecake!" Helen said. "We'll split a piece though."

"Spoilsport!" Hank said dejectedly.

Chapter 10

Helen awoke at six thirty in the morning to fix an early Breakfast since they had a long day ahead of them in their investigation. When she entered the forward area of the motorhome she felt the abnormal chill that hadn't been felt since they returned to the Ochlocknee campground. She immediately checked the window above the kitchen sink for the distelfink but it wasn't there. Glancing across the aisle she saw it hanging once again in the window above the dinette table. Feeling the chill and the rising goosebumps on her arms she turned and looked toward the front of the Bounder and saw the misty figure of a teenaged girl with brown hair.

Helen stood and stared speechless at the apparition for a moment then uttered, "Sarah, we didn't forget. We will know soon."

Apparently satisfied with Helen's remark the apparition of Sarah Payne smiled and faded away. The warmth once again returned to the area.

Hank arose from the bed and walked out into the Bounder's kitchen to see Helen standing and staring into the forward area. "Did I just hear you talking to someone," he asked.

Helen was startled and flinched when she heard Hank behind her and said, "Don't scare me like that Hank."

"I'm sorry; I didn't mean to scare you. Were you just talking to someone?

"Yeah, Sarah was here for an update on our investigation and I told her we will know something soon," Helen answered nonchalantly.

"Let me get this straight, Sarah Payne's ghost was just here and you were talking to her and I was the one to scare you."

"Well you can be a big ogre at times," Helen replied.

"Gee, I always thought of myself as a gentle giant."

"Yes you are, big guy," Helen replied and pecked him on the cheek.

"Ok, now that we got my status corrected, please tell me what just happened this morning."

Helen explained the event to Hank, "I came out to the kitchen to make us breakfast and noticed the distelfink was in the other window. I felt the same chill we felt before, got goosebumps, and turned to see Sarah standing in the forward area. I somehow sensed why she was here and told her that we didn't forget her and we will know something soon. Then she just smiled and faded away."

Hank just replied with a "huh" and then asked, "What are you making for breakfast?"

"Is that all you can say after what I just told you?" Helen asked in exasperation.

"Well, we do have to keep our clients informed," Hank replied with a chuckle.

Helen then broke out into laughter and Hank followed with laughter of his own.

"Scrambled eggs, sausage patties, and hash browns," Helen managed to utter through her laughter.

"Is Miss Payne joining us," Hank asked.

"No, I'm sure Miss Payne left the Bounder," Helen laughingly replied.

Hank was outside emptying the Bounders black water tank into the campgrounds sewer line when ex-sheriff Jim Rainey pulled up at the campsite in his Chevy SUV.

"Good morning Jim, need any coffee?" Hank asked.

"No thanks Hank, I'm good," Rainey replied.

"Ok, as soon as Helen is ready we can head on over to Mrs. Hartman's," Hank no sooner said when Helen came out of the Bounder.

"Good morning Mrs. Moran," Rainey said as Helen approached carrying a zippered type note pad/organizer.

"Good morning sheriff," Helen replied. "I think I have everything we need to make our rounds in the campground. Are we ready to head to Mrs. Hartman's to talk with Eddie?"

"I think we are as soon as I wash my hands," Hank replied.

The trio walked the short distance to Mrs. Hartman's and found her and Eddie sitting on the front porch. "Well good morning Sheriff Rainey, how have you been doing?" Mrs. Hartman asked as the trio stepped up onto the porch.

"Oh I'm doing well," Mrs. Hartman," Rainey said. He then turned to Eddie and said "Good morning Eddie," as he extended his hand.

Eddie stood and pensively shook hands with the ex-sheriff.

"Eddie, this is Mr. and Mrs. Moran," Mrs. Hartman said. "Mr. and Mrs. Moran and Sheriff Rainey would like to talk with you for a few minutes."

"They are the investigators like on TV," Eddie said.

"Yes, they are investigators and would like to ask you some questions about something that happened here at the campground. So let's everybody take a seat and we can begin. I had Eddie bring out some extra chairs," Mrs. Hartman said.

After everyone was seated Hank nodded to Sheriff Rainey as a cue to begin.

"Eddie, we need to ask you some questions about something that happened to a girl many years ago here at the campground. You were just a young fellow then and you might not remember it," Rainey began.

Eddie fidgeted around on his chair, looked down at his hands and said, "I remember the night the girl was murdered."

"Very good Eddie, that's what we need to talk about," Rainey replied. "Someone told us they saw you, after the fireworks were over, on the other side of the lake picking up spent rocket casings. Do you remember that?"

"Eddie fidgeted some more and replied, "Yes, I remember.

Mr. Higgins asked me to find them and put them on a pile."

"Oh, so you were helping to clean up for Mr. Higgins. Very good," Rainey replied. "Now Eddie, I need you to think very carefully. When you were over there cleaning up did you see a girl sitting on the other side of the lake?"

"Yes I saw the girl and waved to her and she waved to me."

"Was the girl sitting by herself," Rainey asked.

"She was talking to someone and then he left," Eddie replied.

"Do you remember who she was talking to?"

"The man with the band with no hair," Eddie replied.

Being careful not to pose any leading questions, Rainey then asked, "How long did the man with the band talk with the girl?"

"It was only a little time and then he left."

As Helen was taking notes she thought it would be a good time to produce the photograph of the band and show it to Eddie. "Eddie this is a picture of the band. Is the man you saw talking to the girl in this picture?"

Eddie pointed to Charles Hewitt on the photo and said, "That's him. That picture is in the office."

Helen glanced at Mrs. Hartman who said, "He's right Mrs. Moran. We took a picture of the band that night and Mike Beasley requested a copy of it since his band was never photographed."

"I see," Helen said. "Mr. Beasley has the same photograph hanging up in his real estate office. Sorry for the interruption Sheriff Rainey, please continue."

"That's ok Ms. Helen," Rainey replied and turned back to Eddie. "Eddie, after the man with the band left did you notice anyone else with the girl?"

Eddie appeared extremely agitated and didn't answer. He looked at his grandmother and reached for her hand. Mrs. Hartman took his hand and said, "Eddie, you don't have to be afraid to answer Sheriff Rainey's questions. Nothing is going to happen to you. You are safe here."

"But he said he would hurt us if I told on him."

"Who said he would hurt you," Rainey asked.

"The man who hurt the girl," Eddie replied.

"Did you see him hurt the girl?" Rainey asked.

"Yes, he grabbed her from behind and made her fall to the ground. Then he jumped on top of her. I hid behind a bush for a while and then ran around the lake. Then the man caught me and asked if I saw what he did. I said yes and then he told me that if I told anyone he would come back and hurt everyone in my family. He let me go and then I ran up to Grandma's house."

"That's quite a story, Eddie. You don't have to be afraid now." Rainey said. "Did you know who the man was?"

"No, but he is in the picture," Eddie replied.

"He's in the picture Mrs. Moran showed to you?" Rainey asked with excitement.

"Yes, the other man with no hair," Eddie replied.

Helen took the picture out of her note pad case and showed it to Eddie. Eddie pointed to a person standing off to the right side and behind the band. Helen looked closely at the picture and saw the person Eddie had pointed at. He appeared to be in his late teens or early twenties and was looking directly at the camera. His head appeared shaven and he appeared to be just walking by plus he seemed to have a surprised look on his face that a picture was being taken.

"Mrs. Hartman, when was this picture taken, it still looked light out," Helen inquired.

"It was taken after the band set up their equipment and before they started playing. And yes, it was still light out," Mrs. Hartman replied. "This was the first year we had rock music instead of country so we wanted to be sure to get a picture for our wall in the office."

"So that means the gentleman in the picture that Eddie pointed out was present most of the evening," Helen stated. "Mrs. Hartman can you look closely at the picture and see if you recognize the person."

Helen handed the picture to Mrs. Hartman who closely scrutinized the photo. "Oh my, my eyesight isn't what it used to be. I don't think I remember anyone who looked like that checking in. If he was with a family he might have stayed in their vehicle while another person checked in. Perhaps the photo on the office wall is clearer. I had it enlarged to an eight by ten."

"May I borrow the photo from the office?" Helen asked.

I would like to scan it and enlarge the area with the mystery man. That way I can show it to the campers we are going to interview today."

"That's a good idea!" Mrs. Hartman said. "Eddie, can you go to the office and bring us the picture?"

Eddie said Ok and headed to the office across the drive. A short time later he returned with the photograph and handed it to his grandmother who in turn passed it on to Helen.

"Thank you, Mrs. Hartman," Helen said as she stood up. "I'm heading back to the Bounder to work on the picture of our mystery man."

Hank said, "Ok, I want to ask Eddie a few more questions. Jim and I will be there shortly to formalize our game plan for the interviews."

Hank turned to Eddie and said, "Eddie did the man you saw hurt the girl ever come back to the campground?"

"No, I didn't see him anymore," Eddie replied.

"Think carefully now Eddie, if you picture in your mind the same man but with hair on his head, did you ever see a man who might look like that?"

Eddie wrinkled up his face and squinted his eyes for a moment then said, "I thought I saw a man like that but he wasn't the same."

"When did you see that man Eddie?"

"When I was younger."

"Ok Eddie, you have been a great help in our investigation," Hank continued. "You take care of your Grandma now and we'll continue looking for the man you saw."

"Ok," Eddie replied.

Hank and Jim Rainey returned to the Bounder just as Helen was finished printing out copies of the cropped band photo showing the shaved head suspect. She handed copies to Hank and Jim and said, "The suspect's face came out pretty good. I was able to sharpen it up a bit."

Jim Rainey perused the photo and said, "This will be really helpful when we question the campers, good job. How many campers do we need to interview?"

"I thought at first the number would be the five that you had mentioned in your case file," Hank replied. "But now with the introduction of the photo, I think we should question all seventeen campers that are here who were also here in two thousand three. Also Mr. Higgins the fireworks vendor."

"You're right, Hank. If we're lucky one of the seventeen might recall the suspect camping right next door. A young person with a shaved head should be easy to remember."

"We'll NEED to get lucky with a case this cold," Hank replied.

"Well, how do you want to handle the interviews? Do we split up or interview them all together?" Rainey asked.

Hank thought a moment and then replied, "I think it's best if the three of us stick together. One of us might think of an important question to ask that the others missed. It will take longer but it will be more thorough."

"I think you are right with us sticking together, Hank. Where do we start? Rainey asked.

Helen had circled the seventeen camper's sites on a campground map that was given to her when they registered at check-in. "I think a good place to start is with the Arnolds back behind us in site three and work our way around the circle and then up to the Weavers in site forty-nine," Helen suggested.

"Ok, let's go," Hank said with growing excitement hoping a solid lead as to the murderer of Sarah Payne will shortly be found.

Chapter 11

The trio walked back around the circle drive and approached four people sitting in lawn chairs outside a large fifth wheel trailer at site number three.

"Good morning folks, I am Hank Moran and this is my wife Helen and retired Sheriff Jim Rainey. We would like to talk with Mr. and Mrs. Arnold if it's not too much of an imposition."

"Well hello Y'all, I'm Jack Arnold and this is my wife Karen. Are you here about the murdered girl back about ten years ago? We heard you might be making the rounds."

"Yes we are," answered Hank. We understand from the campground records and the sheriff's case file that you were present back then."

"Yes, we were here. I remember being questioned by the sheriff's deputy but I'm afraid we couldn't help much."

"Mr. Arnold, according to the case file you testified you saw the campground owner's grandson run past your campsite that night a few minutes before the band quit playing. I know it's been a long time but do you recall telling that to the deputy?" Hank questioned further.

"Yes, I remember, and so does the rest of our little group. We were discussing that night just before you folks walked up. This is Barry Wilmer and his wife Anne. We were camping side by side that weekend just as we are now but over in sites eight and nine not far from the office."

"I see, good to meet you, Mr. and Mrs. Wilmer. You were on our list to talk to also. Since the night of the murder and being questioned by the sheriff's department have any of you recalled further details however slight that might help our investigation."

Mrs. Arnold raised her hand and spoke, "I do recall that Eddie looked really scared and appeared to be crying when he ran past us. He made a beeline for the back office door and hurried inside."

"Thank you, Mrs. Arnold, we do know what happened to Eddie that night and yes he was scared, to put it mildly. Mrs. Moran has a picture of a person we would like you to look at and see if you remember that person in the campground that weekend."

Helen presented a copy of the photo to each couple and said, "Please take a good look at the photo and see if you can recall seeing that person."

Both couples studied the picture and all four were shaking their heads. "The only kid I saw with a shaved head that night was the roadie with the band but this doesn't look like him," Mr. Wilmer said.

"You are correct Mr. Wilmer, he is not the band's roadie," Helen said.

Hank turned to Jim Rainey and said, "Sheriff Rainey is there anything you would like to ask these folks?"

"I would like you folks to keep a copy of the picture and study it some more. Mr. Moran's number is at the bottom and don't hesitate to call if you remember anything at all about that person."

"We'll be sure to do that Sheriff. By the way, do you think this guy is the murderer?" Jack Arnold asked pointing to the person in the picture.

"As of now he is a person of interest, Mr. Arnold," Rainey replied. "Thank you for your help."

The trio walked back to the driveway and Hank said, "Who's next partner?"

Helen briefly scanned her campground map and said, "The Bridges are right up there in site eleven. They were here that weekend but weren't mentioned in Jim's case file so we just need to show them the picture of our mystery man."

They approached an older Winnebago thirty-three-foot Sightseer motorhome parked in site eleven. No one was sitting out so Jim Rainey knocked on the door. A barefoot man in his sixties with a sizeable paunch, wearing brown shorts and a blue Willie Nelson tee shirt, opened the door. He had a half of a sandwich in his hand and peered down and spoke at Rainey as he chewed a bite that was in his mouth, "What are you folks selling? There's no soliciting allowed in the campground."

"Sir we're not trying to sell you anything. I'm sorry to interrupt your lunch. Are you Mr. Bridges?" Rainey asked.

"Yeah?" was Bridges curt reply as he swallowed his bite of sandwich.

"Mr. Bridges, I am Ex-Sheriff Jim Rainey and these folks are from the Moran Investigation Agency. We would like to have a very brief talk with you and your wife."

Bridges answered, "Oh I suppose it's all right. What do you want to talk about?"

"We understand from the campground's records that you were camped here back in two thousand and three when a girl was murdered and we would like you to look at a picture of a person to see if you remember seeing him back then."

Bridges turned and hollered back into the Winnebago, "Rosie come on out here. The police want us to look at a picture."

"Darrell, you don't have to holler. I can hear you. You say the police are here?" Mrs. Bridges queried.

"Yeah, I told you they want us to look at a picture," Darrell replied.

Mrs. Bridges appeared at the side of and slightly behind Darrell. She was a slim middle-aged woman of average height with blond hair neatly pulled back into a ponytail. She had on a pair of expensive looking embroidered white shorts and a light blue top and a pair of white earrings. The couple appeared to fit into two different lifestyles. Helen was amused at the couple's contrasting appearance and thought; *"I guess there is something to that old adage that opposites attract."*

"Darrell, why don't you invite the people in?" Rosie requested.

"That's ok folks, we don't want to interrupt your lunch," Rainey said.

"Oh we're not having lunch," Rosie Bridges replied. "My husband is always chewing on something."

"This will only take a minute," Rainey said as he handed a printout of the suspect to Darrell Bridges. "Now please look carefully at the picture of this individual and try to recall if you saw him back in two thousand and three here at the campground."

Darrell put on his reading glasses which were held by a braided cord around his neck and studied the picture. Rosie pulled Darrell's arm closer to her so she could also study the picture. Darrell was shaking his head but Rosie was nodding hers. "This guy's face really rings a bell," Rosie said faintly as if talking to herself. Then louder she said, "I think this is the guy who tried to pick me up. He was walking towards me as I was walking back to our campsite and he stopped and started talking to me and making passes. He looked a little weird to me. I told him I was married and I hurried away."

"Was this back in 0'three?" Rainey asked excitedly.

"Oh yes, yes it was," Rosie replied.

"Mrs. Bridges, do you recall in which area this event happened?" Helen asked.

"Let me think," Rosie replied. "I was walking back from the shuffleboard and horseshoe area and it happened by that line of campsites near the creek. I don't remember the exact spot."

"You never told me that some guy tried to pick you up," Darrell gruffly said.

"Oh, Darrell, it was nothing, besides if I had said something you would have most likely started something with the guy."

"You're damn right!" Darrell uttered.

Helen checked the campground map to find the numbers of the campsites near where the suspect stopped to talk to Rosie. "The sites mentioned by Mrs. Bridges are numbers thirty-eight through forty-five," Helen said. There is only one registered camper out of the seventeen who was in one of those sites back then and that was a Mr. John Wertz who was in site forty-three and . . . he is now registered in site one-o-six."

"Ok, thank you, you've been a big help Mrs. Bridges," Rainey said. "It looks like we need to have a talk with Mr. Wertz. Thanks again, folks."

The trio walked back and paused in the roadway.

"I think we are getting somewhere!" Hank said. "If Mr. Wertz proves to be of little help we can contact the rest of the campers who were here back then. It's great that Mrs. Hartman kept such good records."

The trio walked around Circle Drive, then onto the main entrance road and right onto Oak Trail to site one-o-six.

As they approached the campsite a brown-haired man dressed in khaki cargo pants and maroon colored tee shirt was busy grilling burgers on a small electric tabletop grill. He looked up when the trio appeared.

"Are you Mr. Wertz?" Rainey asked.

"I'm John Wertz, and who might y'all be?"

"I'm Sheriff Jim Rainey retired and my two associates are from the Moran Investigations Agency."

"Hello Mr. Wertz, I am Hank Moran and this is my wife and agency partner Helen Moran. We'd like to ask you a few questions about the murder of Sarah Payne that happened here in two thousand three. We saw on the campground's records that you were camped here that weekend."

"Yes, I remember that weekend. How can I help you?"

"According to the campground records you were in site forty-three that. We have reason to believe a person of interest was seen near your site. We have a photograph of the person and we would like you to look at it and see if you remember him."

"Sure, let me see it."

When Helen handed Mr. Wertz the photograph he looked at it briefly and smiled. "I think I saw this guy around the campground back then. He walked by our site a few times and stared at my wife. Hold on a minute I'll get her." Wertz went into his travel trailer and re-appeared a minute later. "She'll be out in a minute. She was just changing into her bathing suit."

A moment later Mrs. Wertz stepped out of the travel trailer wearing a multi-colored pool robe and turquoise sandals. Mr. Wertz introduced his blond-haired wife Angela to the Moran's and Sheriff Rainey.

"Angela, Mrs. Moran showed a photograph to me of a person whom I think was here in the campground back when that poor girl was murdered," John Wertz said. "They would like you to take a look at it to see if you remember him."

"Sure, let me see it," Angela Wertz responded.

Helen handed the picture to Mrs. Wertz who briefly studied it and with big eyes said, "This is the creepy guy who kept walking by our camper staring at me. He really made me cringe!"

"Mrs. Wertz, do you remember seeing him at any of the campsites?" Hank asked.

"No, every time I remember seeing him he was walking somewhere by himself."

"Did you see him over the whole weekend or just on the July Fourth holiday?" Helen inquired.

"I am pretty sure that is was only on the day of the fireworks because I remember a feeling of relief that I no longer saw him. I remember saying something to John the next day that I thought the creepy guy was gone."

"That's right, I remember that!" John Wertz said. "In fact, I don't recall seeing him the rest of the weekend!"

Rainey asked Hank and Helen if they had any more questions, and when they said no he told the Wertz's, "Thank you, folks, you've been a big help. If you think of anything else that might help us to identify the person in the photo please don't hesitate to get in touch with Mr. or Mrs. Moran. Their motorhome is in site twenty-two."

"We surely will," John Wertz replied.

The trio walked back to the driveway and held a small confab.

"I have a feeling he was not a registered camper," Helen suggested. "We talked with four couples so far and we failed to place him in a campsite. Maybe we'll have better luck when we talk with the remaining campers on our list, but I believe he was from the outside."

"You may be right Helen but we have to do our due diligence and question the remainder of the campers," Rainey replied.

"Oh, I totally agree," Helen responded. "I wasn't suggesting we stop our interviews. It looks like the Weavers are next on the list and they are around the corner in site forty-nine."

The Weavers provided nothing additional to aid in the identification of the shaved-headed suspect. After a brief tour of their new Bounder Motorhome and refreshing glasses of iced tea, the Weavers bid them good luck in their search and invited them back for a cookout later in the afternoon.

The questioning of the remaining campers proved fruitless in the identification of the mystery man. As they were interviewing the last of the campers Hank spotted a man across the lake who appeared to be setting up the night's fireworks display. "That must be Mr. Higgins over there," Hank said as he pointed across the lake.

"You're right, that is Mr. Higgins," Rainey confirmed.

"I think we should head over there and see what he has to say," Hank suggested.

The trio walked around the short side of the lake and approached Higgins as he was bent over wiring a set of progressively launched rockets. "Mr. Higgins, can we disturb you for a few minutes?" Rainey asked.

Higgins, slightly startled, stood up and turned to the trio, "Well I'll be, Sheriff Rainey, is that you?"

"It sure is Joe, how have you been?" Rainey replied.

"Oh, I can't complain Jim. I didn't recognize you at first without your uniform. What brings you out on this fine day?

"Joe, I'm sure you remember the death of the girl here at the campground eleven years back. I am helping these people from the Moran Investigations Agency to hopefully find the culprit who done it. This is Hank Moran and his wife and partner Helen Moran."

Hank and Helen shook hands with Joe Higgins and then Hank asked, "Mr. Higgins, we have a photograph of a person of interest in the case we would like you to look at and see if you remember seeing him around the campground on that Fourth of July holiday."

"Sure, I'll take a gander," Higgins replied.

Helen handed a copy of the photo to Higgins who looked at it briefly and said with surprise, "If I'm not mistaken that's my sister Hannah's boy. You said he's a person of interest in the case?"

"That's right Joe, do you remember how he came to be at the campground that day."

"If I recall, my other nephew Jake, who is my brother's boy, was helping me out that day. Jake and my sister Hannah's boy Brad get together occasionally and Jake told him about the fireworks and the rock band that was supposed to play that night. Well, Brad showed up in the afternoon and hung around with as for a while as we were assembling the fireworks show. He took off every now and then during the afternoon. Then he heard that the band arrived to set up their amps and stuff and he took off up in that direction. That's the last I saw of him."

"Mr. Higgins, do you know if Jake interacted with Brad at all that evening?" Hank inquired.

"A lot of it is coming back to me Mr. Moran. Yes, I remember letting Jake go to watch the rock band as I was nearly done with the rigging. I told him to high tail it back after the band's first set as I needed him to help set off the fireworks show. I am only assuming he located Brad up by the band."

"Mr. Higgins, what is your nephew Brad's full name and address?" Hank inquired.

"His last name is Culpepper and I am pretty sure he still lives in his mother's place up in Moultrie on Hightower Boulevard. I think the street number is eight twenty. I always knew my sister Hannah's place by sight and never paid much attention to the street number. I lost touch with Brad when Hannah passed on with cancer four years ago. Brad had just come back from the war in Afghanistan and they say he was suffering from PTSD."

"Do you think your nephew Jake might still be in touch with Brad and know if he is still staying at the same residence?" Helen asked.

"I can give him a call and find out," Higgins replied as he pulled out his cell phone from a leather pouch fastened to his belt, scanned his contact list and tapped on Jake's entry."

Jake felt his phone vibrate in his pocket, pulled it out, and saw his Uncle Joe was calling. "Hey Uncle Joe what's up? Need help with the fireworks?

"Hi Jake, no I'm not calling about your helping me tonight. You lost your job a few years ago when I discovered the benefits of a computer."

"That's right, you have most everything automated now Uncle Joe. So this is just a social call?"

"Well, not exactly Jake. There are some investigators here at the campground asking about your cousin Brad. Does he still live up in Moultrie at your Aunt Hannah's place?"

"Yes, he does. Why are they asking about Brad?"

"Maybe its best if you come over to the campground. We're back at the lake where I'm setting up tonight's show."

"Ok Uncle Joe, I was just heading out for a run so I can head over that way. See you in a few."

Higgins ended the call and said, "Jake will be here in a few minutes. He's out for a run and heading this way. I don't see how he does it. He lost the lower part of his left leg to a roadside bomb in Afghanistan and wears one of those prosthetic legs with a spring on the bottom. He gets around really great."

"So, both of your nephews served in the Afghan war?" Helen asked.

"They signed up together right out of high school. Brad didn't want to a first, but Jake talked him into it. He said it would be good for him since he needed a little discipline. Brad was always a little bit of a trouble maker in high school since his father took off and left his mother."

What kind of trouble did Brad get into?" Helen asked.

"He belonged to one of those right-wing gangs that shaved their heads and thought they could rule the school. Mostly bullying type stuff."

Higgins was facing the wooded area behind the lake and saw Jake jogging towards them on the trail. "Here comes Jake now."

The trio turned and watched as Jake approached them. He was wearing shorts and a U.S. Army sweatshirt with the sleeves cut off. His jogging pace looked to be normal even with his left prosthetic lower leg.

When Higgins introduced Jake to Rainey and the Moran's, Hank thanked him for his service.

"So, what did you want to know about my cousin Brad?" Jake asked his Uncle Joe.

"These folks need to ask you about the night the girl was murdered down here by the lake," Higgins answered.

"Wow, that was a long time ago. What do you want to ask me?" Jake asked eyeing no one in particular in the trio."

Rainey was the first to answer, "Jake, I guess we could start off by asking you to look at a photograph to see if you can identify the person in it."

Jake produced a smile when he gazed at the photo that Helen handed to him. "That sure is my cousin Brad, shaved head and all," Jake said with a chuckle.

Rainey proceeded with the questioning, "Jake, your Uncle Joe told us that Brad showed up the afternoon before the girl's murder as you were helping your uncle set up the fireworks show. Do you recall seeing him?"

"Yes, I remember that day. The campground was having a Rock band that night and I called Brad to tell him about it to see if he wanted to come down to hear them. He showed up and hung around with us off and on for a while and then headed up to the stage to watch the band set up their equipment. I met Brad later up near the band's stage when they started to play."

"How was Brad acting at this time? Did he act normal?" Rainey asked.

"Yeah, he was the same old Brad trying to pick up every girl in the area. He particularly keyed in on one girl who in no uncertain terms told him to get lost."

Jake's last remark piqued the interest of the trio, "Do you remember who the girl was that rejected him?" Helen asked.

"No, I don't think she ever gave him her name. I do remember him calling her a bitch though."

"I have another picture I need you to look at," Helen said as she produced a copy of Sarah Payne's picture that was printed in the newspaper eleven years ago. "Would this be the girl who rejected Brad that night?" Helen asked as she handed the picture to Jake.

"Huh, I remember seeing this picture in the newspaper back when she was murdered," Jake said. I thought she looked familiar when I saw it back then but I couldn't quite remember where I saw her. Now that I brought up the incident with Brad and that girl, I'm thinking this might just be her."

"Jake, was Brad with you during the band's entire first set?" Rainey asked.

"Yes, he was," Jake replied. "When the band stopped playing I immediately came back down here to the lake to help Uncle Joe with the fireworks."

"Do you recall seeing Brad anymore that night?"

"Well, when the fireworks were over Uncle Joe drove me home. I live only a quarter mile back over there," Jake said as he pointed back the trail. "When I got home I quickly changed my shirt and pants and headed back to the campground for the band's last set. I looked around for Brad but I couldn't find him. I thought he must have gone home or picked up a girl and went parking. When the band quit I went back over to my house."

"Then you left before the girl's body was found?" Rainey asked.

"That's right, I didn't hear about it until the next day when me and Uncle Joe came back to clean up the spent housings and rocket casings from the fireworks."

"Do you have Brad's phone number?" Rainey asked.

"Sure it's right here in my cell's contact list. I just talked to him."

"You just talked to him?" Rainey asked with concern.

"Yeah, I called him before I came over here. Uncle Joe mentioned there were detectives here at the campground asking about him. I called him and told him about the detectives, and jokingly asked what he had done now."

"How did he react when you told him that?" Rainey asked

"He said he had no idea why detectives were here and said he had to go because he would be late for a date."

"Ok, give me his number," Rainey said.

Jake gave Rainey Brad's cell phone number and said, "I kind of get the drift y'all think Brad had something to do with the murder of that girl."

"Right now your cousin is only a person of interest in the case," Rainey replied not wanting to give Jake too much information in case he made another call to Brad. He also didn't want to mention about a witness to the crime for the same reason.

Rainey thanked Joe Higgins and his nephew for their help and told them that if they happen to remember anything else of importance that would be of help in the case to contact Mr. Moran. Hank handed them both one of his cards and said they could also reach him and Mrs. Moran at their motorhome in site twenty-two.

The trio walked back to the campground side of the lake and held another small confab. "Do you think Brad Culpepper is now a threat to Eddie since he knows we are considering him a suspect?" Helen asked.

"It's hard to say what his state of mind is considering his service in Afghanistan and his PTSD problem. He could possibly consider Eddie a threat, but it's anybody's guess what he would do about it," Hank replied.

"Right now I think the wise thing to do is to sit down with Sheriff Berry and tell him what we have uncovered. He may also want to have a police presence here at the campground just in case Culpepper decides to act on his old threats to Eddie," Rainey suggested.

"I agree with you one hundred percent," Hank said. "Helen has his number in her cell. Let's head back to our motorhome and call him."

When they entered their motorhome Helen out of habit glanced at the window above the sink and noticed the distelfink was missing. She then saw it was once again relocated to the window above the dinette. Not wanting to discuss the charms relocation in front of Sheriff Rainey she asked if anybody could use something to drink. "I have iced tea, lemonade, and beer."

"I sure worked up a beer thirst after all of those interviews but it feels like I'm still on duty," Rainey replied. "I'll just settle for a glass of lemonade."

Hank chuckled at Rainey's remark and said," I'll have some lemonade also, I'd feel bad drinking a beer in front of Jim.

Helen poured the drinks and sat down at the dinette and called Sheriff Berry with the phone's speaker on. The call was transferred from the switchboard to Berry's office.

"Sheriff Berry speaking, how can I help you?"

"Sheriff Berry this is Helen Moran. My husband Hank and I met you a few days ago and told you we were here working on Sarah Payne's murder case."

"Good afternoon Mrs. Moran, how is the investigation going?"

"That's what we need to talk to you about. I have you on speaker and I'm sitting here with my husband and Jim Rainey. Mr. Rainey would like to update you on what we uncovered and request your assistance."

"Ok, hello Jim, what have you got?"

"Shiloh, we turned up a witness to the murder and have a prime suspect. Do you want to discuss this over the phone or should we come down to the station?"

"Hmm, are you up at the campground?" Berry asked.

"Yes, we are. We're in the Moran's motorhome."

"Tell you what, I've been sitting behind my desk all day and feel the need to get out of the office. I'll head up and meet you there if it's alright."

"You're entirely welcome," Helen said. "We're in the black and gold Bounder in site twenty-two."

"Heading right there," Sheriff Berry responded.

Chapter 12

Twenty minutes later Sheriff Berry pulled into a parking space at the campground office and went in and received directions to site twenty-two. It was a short distance to the site so he decided to walk to his destination. Harry and Wilma Schultz were sitting by their camper when Sheriff Berry approached and Wilma said, "Good afternoon sheriff, what brings you up here on this fine afternoon?"

"Just patrolling the area folks and decided to drop in on some friends," Berry replied as he turned and continued his walk up to the Moran's motorhome.

"Watch out for the raccoons," Wilma shouted when she realized Berry's destination.

Berry glanced back towards Wilma with a puzzled look and then knocked on the motorhome's door taking note of the "Moran Investigations Agency" sign.

Hank opened the Bounder's door and greeted Sheriff Berry, "Good afternoon Sheriff Berry, come on in."

Berry's eyes traveled around the motorhome when he entered. "Boy, this is a nice rig. I saw the sign on your door and assume it doubles as your mobile office."

"Greetings Sheriff Berry," Helen said. "Our motorhome started out as only a pleasure vehicle but it seems that every time we take it on the road we get ourselves involved in an investigation."

"Well I guess it does add a little more fun to a road trip," Berry said with a chuckle.

"Believe me, it's not always fun," Helen replied with a smile.

Berry shook hands with Jim Rainey and said, "Well Jim, what have you got on the Sarah Payne case?"

"Hank, do you want to make the presentation," Rainey asked.

"No you go ahead Jim," Hank replied letting the former sheriff take the lead out of respect for Jim's long involvement in the case.

"Okay Shiloh, as I said over the phone, we now have a witness to the crime and a viable suspect. When the Moran's were interviewing the rock band's roadie, a Mr. Charlie Hewitt, he stated he saw Mrs. Hartman's grandson Eddie across the lake fooling with the spent rocket casings. This was just before the band started its last set. We made an appointment this morning to interview Eddie at his grandmother's place. We learned from Eddie that he did witness a man attacking Sarah Payne. The man then caught Eddie and threatened him into silence with threats against him and his grandmother. That was why Eddie said nothing about what he saw all of these past eleven years. Eddie then said there was a picture of the man on the campground's office wall. Mrs. Moran enlarged the man's face and printed out copies to aid in our canvassing of campers who were present that weekend to ask if anyone remembered the person. The fireworks vendor, Joe Higgins, identified the person as his nephew Brad Culpepper who lives up in Moultrie. Culpepper was present that afternoon and evening according to Mr. Higgins and his other nephew Jake Higgins whom we also interviewed. Now, unfortunately, Jake made a call to Culpeper to inform him that detectives were here at the campground asking questions about him. We are now fearful of possible retaliation by Culpepper towards Eddie. We have not tried to contact Culpepper. So, that's about it."

"Ok, sounds like good detective work," Berry said. "How old was Mrs. Hartman's grandson at the time of the murder?"

"He was twelve at the time," Rainey replied.

"Isn't he retarded with some syndrome?" Berry asked.

"Yes, he has Down syndrome," Rainey replied.

"Hmm, how good a witness will he be at a trial?" Berry asked.

"He is very cognizant and would make a very compelling witness and I would not call him mentally retarded," Rainey replied.

"Ok, I guess I need y'all to come down to the station to make a formal statement, and in the meantime, I will inform Chief Leister up in Moultrie that we are interested in one of his citizens."

"Sheriff Berry, we are worried about the safety of Eddie Parks and his grandmother," Hank stated. "Would it be possible to have a police presence here at the campground while we give our statements at your office?"

"Sure, I'll have a deputy park by the campground office while you are gone and when you return please have him radio the dispatcher for further instructions."

"Will do Sheriff and thank you. We'll see you at your office shortly," Hank gratefully replied.

When Sheriff Berry left, Hank asked Rainey, "Jim would you like to ride with us to the sheriff's office."

"No thanks Hank, I need to stop by the house and check on the Missus when we are done so I'll drive myself. I may then head up to Moultrie and have a chat with Chief Leister."

"Ok, we'll see you at the station," replied Hank.

When Hank and Helen were finished giving their statement at the sheriff's office they were walking towards the front door when they were stopped by Sheriff Berry.

"Mr. and Mrs. Moran, before you leave, I just received word from Chief Leister up in Moultrie that they were unable to locate Brad Culpepper at his place of residence. They have a BOLO out on his vehicle and orders to apprehend Culpepper."

"Sheriff, if Culpepper shows up at the campground we only have a ten-year-old grainy photo of him so we don't know what he looks like now," Helen said. "Is it possible to get a photocopy of his driver's license and the make and model of his vehicle?"

"You bet, if you'll have a seat out front, I'll have Deputy Kershaw get you the information."

While Hank and Helen were seated in the reception area Jim Rainey appeared after giving his statement.

"Well folks, I guess we're done here. Did you hear the news from up in Moultrie?"

"Yes, we heard they were unable to locate Culpepper," Hank replied. "We are waiting for a photocopy of his driver's license and the description of his vehicle before we head back to the campground. We're kinda anxious to get back there to check on Eddie knowing Culpepper is on the loose."

Hank no sooner was finished speaking when a tall shapely brunette wearing a deputy's uniform with the nametag Kershaw walked up to them. "Are you Mr. and Mrs. Moran?"

"Yes we are," Hank replied.

"I have copies of the information you requested from Sheriff Berry. Here is a copy of his driver's license photo and the plate number of his 08' blue mustang. I also made an extra copy for Sheriff Jim.

"Thank you, Maggie, Rainey said as the deputy handed him his copy. Maggie, Mr. and Mrs. Moran are from Moran Investigations and they are here working on the Sarah Payne case. They have been a great help. We now have a viable suspect in the case thanks to them." Turning to

Hank and Helen, Jim continued, "Maggie has been with the sheriff's office for over ten years now. She has turned out to be one of my best hires when I was Sheriff."

"Thank you for the help in the case," Maggie said. I know how much bringing the Payne case to a close would mean to Sheriff Jim. I was just a rookie when it happened but I know how frustrating it was for him."

"Well thank you, Deputy Kershaw," Helen replied. "I hope the case will be resolved very soon and we can all get together and celebrate."

Hank and Helen drove back to the campground while Jim Rainey headed home to check on his Missus. When Hank pulled into the campground he stopped beside the Sheriff's Department patrol car which was parked near the entrance, got out, and tapped on the window. The deputy jumped when he heard the tap and rolled down the window. Hank figured he was about to drift off into a nap.

"Can I help you sir?" the deputy said.

"Sheriff Berry asked us to tell you to check in with dispatch for reassignment when we arrive." Hank showed the deputy a copy of Culpepper's photo license and vehicle description. "Did you happen to notice if this gentleman entered the campground during the last two hours? There is now a BOLO out on him from the Moultrie police"

The deputy perused the picture for a brief moment and shook his head. "I received the alert on my radio and I haven't seen the guy or the vehicle."

"Ok, thanks for your help," Hank said as the deputy started his patrol car, backed up, and turned out of the campground.

When he got back into the Honda Hank said, "The deputy said he hasn't seen Culpepper or his car. It looked like he was nodding off to sleep so I don't know how reliable his watch was."

"Let's stop at the office on the way in," Helen said. "I need to check on Eddie and ask Ruth if she might have seen Culpepper."

Hank stopped at the office and asked Helen to go in and talk with Ruth. Hank remained in the Honda to check his phone messages.

Ruth was at the counter when Helen walked into the office. "Good afternoon Helen, how is your investigation progressing?"

"It looks like we are getting somewhere," Helen replied while handing the picture of Culpepper to Ruth. "I would like you to study this picture to see if you might have seen this person enter the campground within the last two hours."

Ruth studied the picture with a wrinkled brow and said, "No I haven't seen him although he does look a little familiar. He looks a little bit like Mr. Higgins would look like in his younger days."

"Funny you should say that," Helen replied. "This just happens to be Mr. Higgin's nephew."

"Hmm, why are you interested in Joe's nephew?" Ruth asked.

"He is a person of interest in the Sarah Payne case. Did you happen to see the blue six-year-old Ford Mustang that he owns pass by the office?" Helen asked.

"No, I haven't seen his car either," Ruth replied.

Helen looked around the office and peered into the lounge area. "I don't see Eddie around, was he here in the last two hours?" Helen asked.

"He was here a short while ago, and then he said he was going down to the lake to see if Mr. Higgins needed any help with the fireworks," Ruth replied.

"Ok, thanks for your help, we'll head down to the lake to try to find him," Helen said.

Hank was checking his phone when Helen reentered the Honda. "I just got a text from Jim; he said he is on the way up to Moultrie to check in with Chief Leister," Hank said.

"Well, we need to go down to the lake to try to find Eddie. Ruth told me he might be down there helping Joe Higgins."

"Ok, we'll park at the Bounder and walk down to the lake. It might be a good idea to show Culpepper's picture around the campground on the way," Hank replied.

Chapter 13

Hank and Helen showed Brad Culpepper's picture to a number of campers on their walk down to the fireworks area. No one recalled seeing the suspect that day.

As they approached the lake they spotted Eddie and Joe Higgins on the opposite side. "Eddie looks ok," Helen said as they walked around the short side of the lake.

"Good afternoon folks," Joe Higgins said as the couple approached. "Did you have any luck in locating my nephew Brad?"

"Not as of yet," Hank replied. "Both the Thomas County Sheriff's department and the Moultrie police are searching for him."

Helen noticed that Eddie was fidgeting nervously in the presence of the two investigators. She assumed he was still apprehensive about revealing the picture of the girl's attacker and still fearful of the attacker's warning to keep quiet about what he had witnessed.

Helen moved next to Eddie and showed him a copy of Brad Culpepper's driver's license photo. "Eddie, this is what the person who attacked Sarah Payne looks like now. If you see this person please run away as fast as you can. Will you do that?"

"I can kick him like the Karate Kid," Eddie replied.

Helen smiled at Eddie's response and asked, "Do you know how to do that."

"I go to class and learn that," Eddie replied.

"You take Karate lessons?" Helen inquired.

"Yes, like Karate Kid."

"Well Eddie, I take Karate lessons too," Helen replied. "But one main thing you learn is to avoid conflict if at all possible and use your skills as a last resort. Did you learn that?"

"Yes, I learned that," Eddie replied looking dejectedly at the ground.

"Good, now what are you going to do if you see this man,"

Helen asked pointing at the picture.

"I'm gonna run like lightning to Grammas house and protect her," Eddie replied.

"That's a much better thing to do," Helen said as she gave Eddie a hug.

"Well, its late afternoon and we haven't had anything to eat since breakfast. Let's head back to the Bounder and see what's in the fridge," Hank suggested.

"I just remembered the Weaver's invited us for a cook-out right about now. Why don't we swing by their site and see what's up?" Helen replied.

"You're right! Good idea!" Hank responded.

The couple decided to walk the short distance to site forty-nine instead of going back to their site and driving. On the way, they showed Culpepper's photograph to any camper they met. No one had seen the suspect. As they approached the Weaver's site, Hank could smell the enticing aroma of fresh hamburger cooking on a barbecue grill.

Carl Weaver greeted them when they entered the campsite, "I am glad you two could make it! We have plenty of burgers on the grille and Rachael whipped up a big batch of her grandmother's recipe of Pennsylvania Dutch potato salad. Why don't you grab a couple of beers or malt coolers and have a seat while I finish these burgers."

Hank chose a Pabst Blue Ribbon twelve ounce long neck from the ice chest and Helen opted for a B&J margarita cooler. Hank and Helen introduced themselves to two other couples who were present for the cookout and took a seat in comfortable canvas folding chairs. "It sure feels good to sit down and relax," Hank remarked as he took a sip from the longneck.

One of the other guests named Martin Hoyer said, "I heard you guys were looking for the guy who murdered the girl ten years ago. Having any luck?"

"The police are presently trying to locate a person of interest," Hank replied. "We have a driver's license photo of him that we've been showing around the campground to see if anybody spotted him here."

"Do you mind if we have a look at it?" Hoyer asked.

"You sure can," Hank replied as he took the enlarged print from his pocket and unfolded it. He handed it to Hoyer and said, "The picture is about two years old and he drives a blue six-year-old Mustang."

Hoyer and his wife Anne briefly studied Culpepper's picture and shook their heads. "We haven't seen him," the Hoyer's said and passed the photo to the other couple whose last name was Morrison. Gary Morrison looked at the photo, shook his head and handed it to his wife Ginger.

Ginger Morrison looked at the picture, shook her head, looked at Hank and asked, "Did you say he drives an older blue Mustang?"

"Yes, a two thousand and eight," Hank replied.

"Gary and I just came back from a long walk to the road back beyond the lake and I remember a blue Mustang passing by as we turned around to walk back to the campground."

"How long ago was this?" Hank asked in excitement.

"Not more than forty-five minutes ago," Ginger replied.

Hank rose and said, "Excuse me, folks, I have to make a phone call."

"He sure got excited when I mentioned seeing that car," Ginger said.

"The person we are looking for has a cousin who lives on that road not far from the campground," Helen said as she rose to join Hank who had walked out to the driveway.

Hank was punching a number into his cell phone when Helen reached him. "Who are you calling?" Helen asked.

"I'm calling Sheriff Berry to have a deputy check out Jake Higgins' place," Hank replied as Sheriff Berry answered the call.

"Sheriff Berry, this is Hank Moran. We just talked to someone who saw a blue Mustang back on Lockerman road. His cousin Jake Higgins lives on that road just behind the campground."

How long ago did the witness see the Mustang?" Berry asked.

"Less than an hour ago," Hank replied.

"Ok Mr. Moran, I'll send two patrol cars back there to see if Mr. Culpepper paid his cousin a visit. I'll get back with you if they turn anything up."

"Thanks, Sheriff, in the meantime we'll check on Eddie Parks to make sure he's safe."

Hank ended the call to Sheriff Berry and tapped on Joe Higgins' number in his directory.

Higgins answered on the fourth ring and rhythmically said, "Hello, this is Joe."

"Joe, this is Hank Moran. Is Eddie still down there with you?"

"Yes, he's right here. You sound alarmed Hank. Is something wrong?"

"Someone spotted a blue Mustang back on Lockerman road less than an hour ago. I'm just being cautious in case Brad Culpepper is in the area," Hank replied.

"I can give my nephew Jake a call to see if he stopped by his place," Higgins suggested.

"No, don't call him Joe. Sheriff Berry is sending a pair of deputies to check Jake's place. I wouldn't want to fore-worn Culpepper if he is there."

"Ok Hank, I'm about finished down here with tonight's show. I'll walk with Eddie up to his Gramma's house in a few minutes."

"Ok, Joe thanks. We'll check on him there later," Hank replied and ended the call. "Ok, now I am going to have one of those delicious smelling burgers and finish my beer."

"Lead the way big guy," Helen responded.

Rachael Weaver had loaded up a folding table with a huge bowl of potato salad, a container of coleslaw, plates of sliced tomatoes, lettuce, green peppers, sweet onions, jalapeno peppers, and an array of condiments. A bowl of tossed salad was also available for the more diet conscious guest. Hank loaded up a burger to treetop level and dug in. Everyone had second helpings of the delicious potato salad.

It was approaching early evening when Hanks cell phone chimed with an incoming call from Sheriff Berry. "Sheriff Berry, did your deputies have any luck locating Culpepper?"

"I'm afraid not, Mr. Moran. Jake Higgins was home and he mentioned his cousin did stop by briefly to ask what the police had on him. Jake told him they wanted to question him in connection with the murder of that girl ten years ago. Culpepper wanted to know how they singled him out and Jake told him they had uncovered a witness. Culpep-per then angrily said, "That damn kid" and took off."

"Did Jake say in what direction Culpepper was headed when he left?" Hank asked.

"He was headed south. We have a four-countywide alert out for his Mustang and to apprehend Culpepper on sight."

"Ok, thanks for the update Sheriff. We're going to stick close to Eddie until Culpepper is apprehended."

"Let us know immediately if you need any assistance up there."

"I will surely do that Sheriff."

Hank and Helen thanked the Weavers for the delicious meal, said goodbye to the Hoyer's and the Morrison's and left to check on Eddie at his grandmother's cottage.

When they arrived at Mrs. Hartman's cottage they were greeted by Mrs. Hartman, Joe Higgins, and Eddie lounging on the front porch.

"Did the Sheriff have any luck in locating my wayward nephew?" Joe Higgins asked.

"Not yet," Hank replied. "The deputies questioned Jake and were told he did show up there but stayed only briefly before taking off in a southerly direction. Unfortunately Jake told Brad that a witness was uncovered. We wanted to keep that information from Jake."

"I'm sorry, I did talk to Jake a while ago and let that bit of information slip," Higgins sheepishly admitted.

"That's too bad Joe, I have a feeling you should call Jake back to check and see if he is ok," Helen said.

"Do you think he might be in danger from Brad?" Joe asked.

"It's just a feeling I have. I'll just feel better knowing that he's ok," Helen replied.

"Ok, I'll give him a call," Joe said as he tapped on Jake's name on his contact's list.

Jake's phone rang six times and went to voicemail, *"You have reached Jake Higgins. I can't answer your call right now so please leave a message."*

Joe waited for the beep and left the requested message, "Jake this is Uncle Joe. Call me back as soon as you can."

Helen's unease continued after Joe's failure to contact his nephew.

Hank's phone chimed a moment later and he saw it was Jim Rainey calling, "Hello Jim, what's up?"

"Hank, I'm heading down that way and should be there in ten minutes. I've been in contact with Sheriff Berry and he told me about Culpepper being down in that area. Chief Leister up in Moultrie couldn't locate Culpepper in his bailiwick."

"It looks like we're on about the same page, Jim. We're at Mrs. Hartman's place now but will be heading to our motorhome shortly."

"Is Eddie there with you," Rainey asked.

"He's safe and sound here with his gramma and Joe Higgins."

"Ok, good to hear. See you shortly," Rainey replied and ended the call.

"I hear the band starting to set up," Hank remarked. "When are they scheduled to start?"

"They should begin playing around eight," Mrs. Hartman replied.

"Joe, when is your fireworks scheduled to start?" Hank asked.

"My show is due to begin at nine sharp," Higgins replied.

"Sounds like the same schedule as eleven years ago," Hank surmised. "I assume the show lasts for a half hour and then the band plays from nine-forty-five till ten-thirty."

"That's what we have planned," Mrs. Hartman replied.

"Ok folks, we're going to head down to our motorhome to wait for Jim Rainey. And Joe, let us know if you connect with your nephew Jake."

"Will do," Higgins replied.

Chapter 14

When Helen entered the Bounder she dialed Betty Hamilton on her cell phone. Betty answered on the fourth ring, "Hello, this is Betty Hamilton."

"Hello Betty, this is Helen Moran. I'm calling to give you an update on our investigation and to ask you a few questions."

"I'm glad you called. How is the investigation going?"

"We have a prime suspect for Sarah's murderer but we haven't been able to locate him as yet. It turned out there was a witness to the crime who was threatened by the suspect not to talk. The witness hasn't said anything about it for eleven years. And now that he came forth we are fearful the suspect might do him harm."

"Does the suspect know the witness came forth?" Betty asked.

"I am afraid so," Helen answered. "The witness is the campground owner's grandson who has Down syndrome. We will be keeping a close watch on him this evening to make sure he remains safe."

"I see. You mentioned that you had some questions for me. How can I help you?" Betty inquired.

"Sarah's spirit has made a few appearances in our motorhome since we started the investigation. There was an occasion or two where she just moved the distelfink from one window to the other but on one other occasion, I could actually see her. I spoke to her and told her we would know something soon. She smiled and then just vanished. My husband Hank and I joked that she appeared for a client update. My question is: How cognizant would she be of our progress and could she actually pick up on who the suspect is from our conversations around the campground?"

"You asked a very good question, Helen. I would venture to say that Sarah is very aware of her surroundings. After all, she did see your agency sign on your motorhome and through a little determination made you aware of her. I was just the medium who made her wishes known to you. As far as picking up on who your suspect is, I would have to come down there and try to connect with her again and ask her." "Once our suspect is apprehended and we are certain he is guilty, what would be the best thing to do as far as her parents are concerned?" Helen asked.

"I am sure Sarah would want to try to communicate with them before she completes her journey to the other side. I am willing to come down there to be the medium if her parents are willing," Betty responded.

"That would be great and it would make a very interesting chapter in your planned book," Helen said.

"Yes indeed it would," Betty replied.

"We would love to have you come down Betty! When do you think you can make it?" Helen replied with excitement.

"Tomorrow is Saturday so both my daughter and I are free. We should be able to make it by noon."

"You are welcome to stay with us in our motorhome." Helen offered. "We have an extra sofa bed that should fit you and your daughter."

"I appreciate the offer but I have an aunt down there in Thomasville who has been begging us to pay a visit. She would be extremely upset if we didn't stay with her," Betty replied.

"Ok Betty, give us a call when you arrive here and get settled. We are looking forward to your help.

"Will do and good look in capturing your suspect. I'll see you tomorrow."

Hank heard the last part of Helen's phone conversation when he entered the Bounder. "I got the gist of your conversation with Ms. Hamilton and I wonder who would be the best person to contact Sarah's parents?" Hank queried.

"That's something we will have to discuss with Jim Rainey and Sheriff Berry," Helen replied. "By the way what happened to you? I thought you were right behind me."

"I kind of got cornered by the Schultz's. They wanted to know what was going on. Word got around the campground that we were looking for a suspect. I told them the police were handling it and that they haven't given us an update."

Just then there was a knock on the door and Hank opened it to welcome Jim Rainey into the Bounder.

"Evening folks, I just checked in with Mrs. Hartman and Eddie is with her and Joe Higgins. Joe said he has to go down to stay with his fireworks to make sure no kids fool around with them. I told them I would go back and stay with Mrs. Hartman and Eddie when Joe leaves."

"Did Joe mention if he had any luck in contacting his nephew Jake?" Hank asked.

"He didn't mention it. I'll ask him when I go back to Mrs. Hartman's," Rainey replied. "Well, I hear the band starting to tune up. They'll be playing soon so I better get back up there to relieve Joe."

"Okay Jim, We're gonna make a few phone calls then patrol around the campground in case Culpepper decides to show up," Hank replied.

"I'm going to try Jake Higgins' number," Helen said. "I'd feel better if I knew he was okay." Helen punched her cell phone's entry for Jake Higgins; it rang six times and went to voicemail. "Jake this is Helen Moran. Give me a call as soon as you can. Call the 504 number in your call log."

Hank heard Helen leave the message in Jake's voice-mail. "Hmm, still no answer from Jake Higgins," Hank said. "I'm going to give Sheriff Berry a call to see if they are having any luck in locating Culpepper."

Hank tried calling Sheriff Berry but he also got a voicemail request to leave a message. "Sheriff Berry, this is Hank Moran. Would you please return my call at your earliest convenience?"

"Well partner, what do you say we start our patrol of the campground? I heard there's a food truck up by the bandstand and I detected the distinct aroma of pork barbecue."

"Sounds good to me," Helen replied. "We can check in at Mrs. Hartman's on the way."

The couple greeted Mrs. Hartman, Eddie, and Jim Rainey who were sitting on Mrs. Hartman's front porch when they arrived. Helen asked Jim Rainey if Joe Higgins was able to get in touch with his nephew Jake.

"Joe tried calling him before he left for his fireworks staging area," Rainey replied. "He seemed upset that Jake hasn't been answering his phone. He said he's kind of a junkie with his phone and always has it in hand."

"I tried to call him also but got his voicemail," Helen added with a worried look on her face.

Eddie was silently taking in the conversation about Jake Higgins and then said, "I like Jake. He let me help with the fireworks. I know where he lives on the road back through the trees. I went there with him one time to see his army pictures."

"Eddie, when did you do this?" Mrs. Hartman asked.

"It was a few years ago," Eddie replied.

"Eddie, you know your mother doesn't want you to leave the campground," Mrs. Hartman sternly said.

"That's okay Gramma. I'm grown up now," Eddie proudly replied.

"Yes, I guess you are. I keep forgetting that fact," his gramma replied.

Hank's cell phone chimed and seeing it was Sheriff Berry he stepped off the porch to answer it. "Hello Sheriff, this is Hank."

"Hello Hank, I'm calling to give you an update on Culpepper such as it is. We have not been able to locate him or his blue Mustang. We are thinking about widening the alert to include the Florida panhandle."

"That might a wise thing to do," Hank replied. "He could stay hidden down there among the beach crowd. What are the chances of posting another deputy at the campground in case he tries something here with Eddie Parks?"

"I could send Deputy Kershaw over there if that would help," Berry replied.

"That would be fine Sheriff. Have her check in at Mrs. Hartman's bungalow when she gets here. Jim Rainey is with Mrs. Hartman and Eddie for now. Mrs. Moran and I will be patrolling around the campground in case Culpepper decides to come here. If he tries anything he might wait for the cover of the fireworks display."

"Okay Hank, Deputy Kershaw should be there within the hour."

"Thanks, Sheriff, give us a call if you apprehend Culpepper."

"Will do Hank."

Hank stepped back onto the porch after the call from the sheriff. "The sheriff's department had no luck in locating Culpepper as yet," Hank informed everyone. Sheriff Berry is sending Deputy Kershaw to help us out."

"All right!" Rainey said, "It will be a pleasure working with Maggie again."

Hank turned to Helen and said, "Okay partner, let's go get a couple of those barbecues and then start our patrol."

The country band was in full swing with a not too bad rendition of "The Devil Went Down to Georgia" as Hank and Helen ordered their barbecues from the food truck. They managed to find an empty spot on a nearby picnic table to enjoy their quick meal and listen to the music. "Not a bad fiddle player," Hank said. "Not quite as good as Charlie Daniels but close."

"Good barbecues too. Are you going to eat that slice of pickle?" Helen asked as she reached for it and stuffed it into her barbecue.

"Why did you even ask?" Hank replied with a chuckle.

They enjoyed their barbecues while keeping their eyes on the meandering crowd in the bandstand area for a possible sighting of Brad Culpepper. When they finished eating they leisurely patrolled through the campground stopping occasionally back at Mrs. Hartman's bungalow to check on Eddie. Deputy Kershaw had arrived and was seated by Jim Rainey. With the presence of the deputy and retired sheriff Rainey, Hank and Helen felt confident of Eddie's safety.

The band finished their first set and announced for everyone to head down to the lake for the fireworks display that was scheduled to begin in ten minutes. Eddie excitedly jumped up out of his chair and said "Let's go! We need to get a good spot."

"Wait just a minute young man," his gramma pleaded. "Deputy Kershaw and Mr. and Mrs. Moran will accompany you."

Eddie grabbed the hand of Deputy Kershaw and helped to pull her out of her chair. "Looks like we better get going folks," the deputy laughingly said as she and Eddie headed down the short set of stairs.

Hank and Helen had to walk briskly to keep up with Eddie who soon stopped and claimed his favorite spot on the bridge spanning the small stream that fed into the lake. Hank liked the viewing spot as it was elevated about two feet above the rest of the viewing area affording him a good view of the crowd.

Joe Higgins started his fireworks show with a rocket that spiraled high into the sky and burst into a multi-colored cascading umbrella. The crowd responded with oohs and aahs as the show continued for the next fifteen minutes with rocket and mortar aerial displays and ended with a loud booming exploding rocket and ground display replica of a red white and blue American flag. Joe Higgins turned on a bright lantern, waved it signaling the end of the show, and bowed to the crowd back across the small lake. The crowd gave him lengthy applause before returning to their camping activities.

The aerial displays had afforded ample light for the Moran's and Deputy Kershaw to survey the surrounding crowd for the possible appearance of Brad Culpepper but Culpepper remained a no-show.

After the fireworks display, Hank and Helen accompanied Deputy Kershaw and Eddie back to Mrs. Hartman's bungalow. Mrs. Hartman and Jim Rainey were sitting on the front porch when they arrived.

"I assume from your laid back approach that y'all had no luck in spotting Culpepper," Rainey said. "All was quiet up at this end except for a few blasts from the fireworks."

"We kept scanning the crowd but didn't spot him," Deputy Kershaw said.

"Helen and I are going to walk back down to try to find Joe Higgins," Hank said upon hearing the country band start its last set. "We need to ask him if he was able to contact his nephew Jake."

Eddie was aware of everyone's concern about not being able to contact Jake Higgins. He rose from his chair on the front porch, whispered to his Gramma that he had to use the bathroom, and entered the bungalow.

Meanwhile, Hank and Helen started their walk down to the fireworks staging area to talk to Joe Higgins. As they approached the far side of the lake they saw Joe busy rolling up his many wire leads and storing them in a large plastic container.

"Hello Joe, nice fireworks display," Hank greeted.

"Thank you, Hank! My new electronics sure help to make the display easy. I am almost finished packing up and was going to stop by Mrs. Hartman's on the way out. Based on your cheery hello I assume Eddie is safe and well protected."

"We left him in the company of his Gramma, Jim Rainey, and Deputy Kershaw, so I think he is quite safe," Hank replied.

"We came down to ask you if you were able to contact Jake since we last talked," Helen inquired with concern in her voice."

"No, as a matter of fact, I haven't. I'll try again right now," Joe said as he tapped on Jake's entry in his phone's list of contacts. Joe had his phone on speaker and everyone heard Jakes phone go to voicemail after six rings. "Darn, I wonder where that boy is. This isn't like him," Joe said after leaving another call back message.

"Joe, does Jake still live with his parent's?" Helen asked.

"Yes, he still lives with my brother and his wife. Jake wanted to head out on his own when he was discharged from the hospital at Fort Benning but my brother Frank convinced him to stay at home till he was fully recovered from the loss of his leg. He's lived there ever since."

"Did you try calling your brother Frank to see if he knows where Jake is," Helen asked.

"No, I haven't. Frank and Mildred left two weeks ago on an extended tour out west. They also have a motorhome and have been putting lots of miles on it in the last few years. I guess that's one of the reasons Jake keeps living at home. He does a lot of upkeep around the place while his folks are traveling and gets to live his own life quite frequently."

"Ok Joe, we're going to head back up to Mrs. Hartman's to check on Eddie and plan with Jim Rainey and Deputy Kershaw what we should do next," Hank said.

"I'll be heading up there shortly also," Joe replied.

Chapter 15

As Hank and Helen approached Mrs. Hartman's front porch they noticed Eddie wasn't sitting in his usual seat. In an apprehensive voice, Hank asked, "Hi everyone, where's Eddie?"

"Oh he went in to go to the bathroom when y'all left to go talk with Mr. Higgins," Mrs. Hartman replied seemingly unconcerned.

"That was over twenty minutes ago and he didn't come back out?" Hank replied questionably.

"I'm sorry; I didn't realize it's been that long. I'll go in and check on him," Mrs. Hartman said now sounding worried.

Mrs. Hartman walked through the small living room and glanced into the kitchen not seeing Eddie. She walked down the short hall and saw the bathroom ajar, "Eddie are you in there?" Not hearing a reply she pushed the door open to find an empty bathroom, "Hmm, maybe he went to bed already." She stepped across the hall and knocked three times on the spare bedroom door where Eddie slept during his visits. "Eddie are you in there?" she questioned once again with more anxiety in her voice. Once again not hearing a reply she opened the bedroom door to find the room empty. "Oh my, where is that boy?" she said as she started to make her way through the bungalow to go back out to the front porch. She glanced into the kitchen once again and spotted a piece of paper on the kitchen counter. Picking it up she noticed it was a note printed in Eddie's block lettering that read, *"GRAMMA WENT TO CHECK ON JAKE."*

Mrs. Hartman rushed out to the front porch and shouted, "He's gone and left a note saying he went to go check on Jake!"

"He must have snuck out the back door knowing we would try to keep him here," Rainey said. "He must have heard us talking about our concern of not hearing back from Jake."

Just then Joe Higgins, on his way to get his truck in order to load up his fireworks gear, approached the group and asked, "Did I just hear someone mention Jake's name?"

"Yes you did," Hank replied. "Apparently Eddie snuck out the back door and is on his way to Jake's house to check on him."

"I just came up from that way and didn't see him. I'll bet he went around the other side of the lake so I wouldn't spot him.

I can get my truck and run over there to check on him," Joe said.

"Hold on, let's talk about this first," Deputy Kershaw interrupted. "We received the report that our deputies questioned Jake a few hours ago. He stated that Culpepper was there and left again, but what if he didn't leave and was holding Jake under duress. I think we should approach Jake's house on foot. If Culpepper is there and hears a vehicle approaching he might panic and put Jake and Eddie in more danger."

"Now, one of us needs to stay here with Mrs. Hartman," Deputy Kershaw stated in taking charge. "Mr. Higgins, you know which house is Jakes and how to get there on foot. Mr. and Mrs. Moran should come along to help in the surveillance of the house. Sheriff Jim, would you stay here with Mrs. Hartman?"

"I'd hate to miss all the action, Maggie. But like I told these folks you were my best hire when I was sheriff, so I trust you can handle things. Sure, I'll stay back here with Mrs. Hartman," Jim replied.

"Ok, one more thing before we head over there, let's put our cell phones on conference so we can use them to communicate if we need to split up," Deputy Kershaw said.

Everyone gave Deputy Kershaw their cell numbers and she adeptly programmed her phone for the conference call. "Now, put your phones on vibrate, we wouldn't want to alert Culpepper with a ringing phone.

Joe Higgins led the group down past the lake and onto the well-worn footpath leading from the campground property to Lockerman Road. He pointed across the road and to the left, "That's Jake place over there. It's the yellow house with the large garage behind it. My brother built the garage to store his motorhome when not in use."

"Ok, here's what we do, I'm going to set up our phones now. Thankfully we have at least four bars reception," Deputy Kershaw said.

The Moran's and Joe Higgins phone vibrated with the incoming call. Everyone confirmed the conference connection including Jim Rainey seated up at Mrs. Hartman's front porch.

"To keep our phone communications as short as possible, we will use first names only," Kershaw instructed. "Now, Joe, I want you to stay here to keep watch in case Culpepper is here and tries to make a hasty exit. We need to know in which direction he's headed. Hank, I need you to make your way back behind the house to the garage and check to see if Culpepper's Mustang is parked in there. Meanwhile, Helen and I will approach the front of the house and wait behind that tall hedge alongside the road."

The trio made their way, thanks to a bright moon, across the road and to the left to the corner of Jakes property. Hank saw an F150 parked in the driveway and spoke into his phone, "Joe, what vehicle does Jake drive."

"He has a burgundy F150," Joe responded from the other side of the road.

"Okay, Jakes truck is here. I'm heading back to the RV garage," Hank replied.

Hank followed the well-worn dirt driveway back to the large garage and quietly approached the building. The garage had a pair of large swing open type doors plus a smaller personnel door with a small window. He didn't want to risk using his cell phones light app in front of the building which would be visible to the house. On checking the left side of the building he found a small dirt encrusted window. He wiped a small area of the glass clean and peered through. The interior of the garage was large and not enough light was available to expose much of the inside, although he thought he could make out a blue shape. Checking to make sure the light wouldn't be visible from the house; he tapped the flashlight app on his phone and held it close to the window. Hank had to clean another small area of the glass beside the phone in order to look through. The phone's light was just strong enough to reveal a 2008 blue Mustang.

Hank talked just above a whisper into his phone, "Maggie, blue Mustang confirmed in the building."

"We read you, Hank. If you can, make your way to the side of the house and see if you can see anything in the windows," Deputy Kershaw requested.

"Will do Maggie," Hank responded.

Hank stepped lightly to the rear corner of the house. There was a back porch with wood decking that he dared not set foot on. He was afraid squeaking boards could be heard inside. There was a side window near the rear that he could silently approach. He kept his back to the wall and took a quick sideways look into the room which turned out to be the kitchen. He was sure nobody was in the room. Another quick look confirmed no one was indeed in the room. However, there was a flickering light that shone through an open doorway from an adjacent room. He assumed a television was playing in the adjacent room although he couldn't hear sound from it.

"Maggie, this is Hank. No one is in the rear kitchen but I think a television is playing in an adjacent room. They must have the sound turned low to be able to hear anyone approaching. I'm moving to the next window."

"Roger that Hank. We can see you now. Be careful," Kershaw replied.

Hank ducked below the kitchen window and inched toward the next window that was emanating some light.

"I am going to call for some backup on my radio but we're too close to the house," Kershaw whispered to Helen. "You stay here. I am going to backtrack a hundred feet and make the call."

Deputy Kershaw crouched low and backed off to across the road and met again with Joe Higgins. "I heard Hank say that he spotted Brad Culpepper's car in the garage," Higgins said.

"Yes he did," Maggie replied. "We haven't spotted Brad as yet. I'm calling for backup as a precaution. Do you happen to know Jakes house number?"

"Yes, it is five-twenty-eight," Higgins replied.

Kershaw took her radio off mute, turned the volume on as low as functionally possible and pressed the talk button. "This is Deputy Kershaw. I need backup at five two eight Lockerman Road. Suspect Culpepper possibly on premises. No lights or sirens. Secure a hundred-yard perimeter and approach on foot. Maintain silence. Over."

"Copy that Kershaw. Help on the way" was the response on her radio.

"Ok Joe, I'm going back over there. Keep watch but don't engage," Deputy Kershaw instructed.

"Are you sure I can't help? He is my nephew," Higgins asked.

"First we have to verify that he is over there Joe. Keep your cell phone on and we'll let you know," Maggie said as she started back across the road.

As Maggie was again approaching the house she spoke into her cell phone, "Are you there Hank?"

"Yes Maggie," Hank whispered. "I heard you back off to call for backup so I didn't want to risk further action till you returned. I am below the next window ready to risk a look-see."

"Proceed, Hank," Maggie replied.

Hank stood up with his back to the wall and edged close to the window. He could hear the muted sounds of a TV program with his ear to the wall. He took a sideways glance through the window and saw Culpepper sitting in a chair along the inside front wall brandishing a handgun. He ducked down again and moved to the other side of the window to get a better look at the rest of the room. Standing up again he took a quick look and spotted Jake Higgins and Eddie sitting side by side on a burgundy colored sofa. Hank ducked down again and whispered into his phone. "Culpepper is armed with a handgun and is seated along the front wall to your left of the front door. Jake and Eddie are seated on a sofa facing him and the front wall."

"Copy that Hank, stand down. We're waiting for backup," Maggie replied.

Helen, who has been hiding behind the roadside hedge with Maggie whispered, "I can make out the knob on the front door. It is to the right. That means Culpepper will be hidden behind the door if you try to rush in."

"Good thinking Helen, we need some kind of distraction to move him away from the door," Kershaw suggested. "I wish I knew if the front door was locked."

Seemingly in answer to her wish, a pickup truck with its bright lights on approached at a high rate of speed from the south. The driver, upon seeing two people crouched behind a hedge close to the road, laid on his horn and sped on by.

Brad Culpepper flinched when he heard the horn, unlocked the front door, opened it, and peered outside. He didn't notice anything out of the ordinary and thought it must have been kids celebrating the fourth. Hank had moved back to the other side of the window and observed Culpepper close the door again. He left the door unlocked.

Hank spoke softly into his phone, "Maggie, Culpepper just closed the front door. The door is unlocked."

"Copy that," Maggie replied.

Across the road, Joe Higgins heard the exchanges between the Moran's and Deputy Kershaw on his cell phones conference connection. He knew police backup would most likely include snipers to take out his nephew if things escalated. Thinking he could talk some sense into his nephew he crossed the road and snuck through the next door neighbor's property to the rear of his brother's house. He stepped quietly up onto the back porch and tried the doorknob. It turned freely in his hand. Finding the door unlocked he talked softly into his cell phone, "Maggie, this is Joe Higgins; I'm at the back door. I'm sure I can talk Brad into giving up."

"Mr. Higgins, please standby and wait for backup," Maggie ordered.

"Sorry Maggie, I'm going in," Higgins replied as he slowly opened the rear kitchen door.

"Well, it looks like we got the distraction you said we needed," Helen said to Maggie.

"Damn it," was the only reply from the deputy.

Joe Higgins entered the kitchen and firmly closed the door hoping Brad would hear it and shouted, "Brad, this is your Uncle Joe, I'm coming in. Please put your gun down."

"I can't do that Uncle Joe. Is there anyone else with you?

"No Brad it's just me and I'm unarmed."

"Ok, come in slowly," Culpepper instructed.

Joe Higgins entered the room with his hands held at shoulder height and pleaded, "Brad please give up. A sheriff's deputy is outside and backup has been called. You can only get yourself in deeper. Please put the gun down and let me call the deputy in."

"I'm sorry Uncle Joe. I am not doing to Jail."

"Brad the police will no doubt have a sniper team who will not let you harm anyone else," Joe Higgins pleaded.

"I'm not afraid to die Uncle Joe. I'd rather have them kill me here than go to jail. I came close to dying many times in Afghanistan. I saw some of my best friends shot up with enemy fire over there but somehow I survived. There have been many days I wished I would have joined them."

Brad's cousin, Jake Higgins, who has been sitting on the sofa beside Eddie pleaded, "Brad listen to me. I've been trying to tell you for the last three hours that help is available for your PTSD. The people at the army hospital helped me through a very difficult time after I had my leg blown off. I wanted to die there in the hospital but the doctors convinced me I had everything to live for."

"I'm really glad for you Jake," Brad replied. "But you don't have a murder charge facing you. The only thing I have to look forward to is spending the rest of my life in prison."

Maggie spoke into her cell phone, "Hank, watch what Culpepper does when I call out to him."

"Go for it," Hank replied.

"Brad Culpepper, this is Sheriff's Deputy Maggie Kershaw. Put your weapon down and come outside with your hands up."

"I can't do that," Culpepper shouted back. "Don't come any closer or people will get hurt. I'm taking the Parks kid with me out the back to my car. Don't try to stop me."

"The sheriff's department has the road blocked you won't get anywhere Brad," Maggie shouted.

"Tell them to back off or the kid gets hurt," Culpepper replied as he pulled Eddie out of his seat on the sofa, moved behind him, put his left arm around Eddie's neck, and put the gun to his head. Culpepper's actions were observed by Hank.

"Culpepper has a gun to Eddie's head," Hank warned in his cell phone. "I'm going around to the back." Hank bolted to the rear of the house and paused beside the back door.

Maggie made the decision to enter the house and confront Culpepper. "Stay here Helen, I'm going in to end this," Maggie said as she rose and walked swiftly to the front door. Drawing her Glock 19 service pistol she turned the doorknob and entered the front room. In a fluid motion, she aimed the pistol at Culpepper.

Culpepper had already had his army issue M9 Beretta aimed at the front door with his left arm locked tightly around Eddie's neck.

"I told you to back off deputy," Culpepper warned once again putting the gun to Eddie's head.

"Don't do this," Joe Higgins pleaded.

"It's too late Uncle Joe," Culpepper replied. "Move over there to the sofa beside Cousin Jake.

Not wanting to risk Eddie's life Joe Higgins obeyed the order and carefully sat down on the sofa beside his nephew.

"Okay, now I'm gonna back out of here," Culpepper said still holding his gun to Eddie's head.

Hank had managed to enter through the back door while Culpepper was distracted by Maggie. He quietly made his way to one side of the doorway between the kitchen and living room and stood with his back to the wall with the intention of disarming Culpepper when he appeared with Eddie. He had noticed while observing Culpepper through the window that he kept his trigger finger on the trigger guard instead of the trigger. Hank was praying this was still the case.

Culpepper was distracted again when Helen entered through the front door and stood beside Maggie. "Helen, I told you to wait outside," Maggie said in exasperation.

"It's ok, I think we have a friend approaching," Helen said with goosebumps growing on her arms.

A sudden chill was felt in the room as Culpeper's mouth dropped open and his eyes widened staring in disbelief at the apparition of a teenaged girl appearing out of a mist in front of Maggie and Helen. The girl had disheveled hair, torn clothing, and bruise marks on her neck. Culpepper now stunned with watery eyes immediately knew who the girl was. "IT'S HER," was all he said as he loosened his grip on Eddie and involuntarily dropped his gun hand down by his side.

Eddie wasted no time in moving behind Culpepper and with an accurately placed karate kick, knocked the gun from Culpepper's hand. The gun went skidding toward the front door but was quickly picked up by Helen.

Hank saw Eddie kick the gun from Culpepper's hand, and rushed into the room. He placed a forward kick behind Culpepper's left knee that sent him buckling to his hands and knees. Maggie moved in, completed the takedown, and deftly cuffed Culpepper's arms behind him.

Sheriff Berry arrived at the scene as Maggie was cuffing Culpepper. "Nice work Kershaw, but what in the hell just happened. As I approached the house I could see Culpepper through the front window. He just stood there seemingly in a daze and lowered his gun. The next thing I saw was you cuffing him when I came in."

"I really can't explain what happened, Shiloh. I felt a sudden chill in the room, Culpepper's mouth dropped open, and his eyes went wide, lowered his gun hand, and shouted: "It's her". Next thing I knew Eddie kicked the gun out of his hand and Mr. Moran subdued him."

"What did he mean by "It's her"," Sheriff Berry asked.

"I'm not quite sure," Maggie answered. "I thought he was looking at Mrs. Moran when he said it.

"He wasn't looking at me," Helen coyly said.

Eddie grinned and said, "He was looking at the girl."

"Eddie, what do you mean, he was looking at the girl?" Maggie questioned.

"He was looking at the girl he hurt!" Eddie answered emphatically.

Maggie just stood there opened mouthed.

Helen smiled while listening to Eddie. She saw Hank give her a questioning look and she silently mouthed "Our Client" to him. Hank just smiled and nodded his head.

As two more deputies named Baker and Hannity arrived on the scene, Sheriff Berry said, "Okay folks, let's wrap this up. Baker and Hannity please escort Mr. Culpepper to a cell and read him his rights. Deputy Kershaw, I will need a full report in the morning. Mr. and Mrs. Moran, if you would stop by my office in the morning and explain a few things with regards to your client I would appreciate it."

"Our client?" questioned Helen.

"I can read lips, Mrs. Moran," Sheriff Berry replied.

"We'll be more than happy to stop by Sheriff," Hank offered not wanting Helen to further comment on their client.

"Okay, I need to pick up my patrol car at the campground office," Maggie said. "We have five people who need a ride."

"Maggie, it's only a short distance back to the campground. Why don't we all walk? I am sure you'll have some questions to ask along the way," Helen suggested.

"You folks go on ahead," Joe Higgins said. "I'm staying here with Brad for a while. I'll get him to drop me off at the campground and help me load my equipment."

Hank, Helen, Maggie, and Eddie left Jake's house and began the walk back to the campground. "That was a brave thing you did when you kicked the gun out of Brad Culpepper's hand," Helen praised Eddie.

"I used a kick I learned in Dojo," Eddie replied. "He made me mad when he called me a kid. I'm grown up now."

"Yes you are, and you're a fine young man," Helen replied.

Eddie reached out and took Helen's hand and said, "I'll help you through the woods so you don't trip and fall Mrs. Moran."

"Why thank you, Eddie," Helen replied with a glad heart.

"Eddie, what did you mean when you said Brad Culpepper saw the girl he hurt?" Maggie asked.

Eddie shrugged his shoulders and said, "He saw the girl. I saw her too. I saw her down at the lake sometimes too."

"Do you mean you saw Sarah Payne, the girl that was murdered here?" Maggie questioned.

"Yes," was Eddie's brief reply.

"Well this is a first for me," Maggie replied. "I've never run across something like this in my eleven years as a deputy."

"Maggie, I'm afraid there is a lot more to the story," Helen said. "Why don't you make yourself available to sit in when we debrief Sheriff Berry on our investigation tomorrow morning?

"I wouldn't miss it for the world," Maggie replied.

Mrs. Hartman and Jim Rainey were waiting on Mrs. Hartman's front porch when the group arrived. Eddie ran up the short stairway and hugged his Gramma saying, "I'm sorry if I worried you Gramma, but I had to go and check if Jake was okay."

"It's okay Eddie, I was angry with you at first but then I realized you are grown up now and you are allowed to make decisions on your own."

"I love you Gramma," Eddie replied and hugged her again.

"That was quite an adventure you guys were on," Jim Rainey said. "Everyone in your party still had their cell phones on in conference in addition to me, and I could hear a lot of what was happening including the conversation during the walk up here. Now, what was all the talk about seeing, I presume, an apparition of Sarah Payne."

"It wasn't just all talk Jim," Helen replied. "I don't know if you are willing to believe, but Sarah's spirit did appear and her appearance helped to put an end to the standoff with Brad Culpepper."

"You have witnesses who actually saw Miss Payne's spirit?" Rainey skeptically questioned.

"Well, I for one saw her and Culpepper must have seen her. That's why he shouted 'It's her' and released Eddie," Helen replied.

"I saw her too!" Eddie said matter-of-factly.

"Well ain't that something!" was Rainey's only reply.

"Well I know some strange things have been happening around the campground since the girl was murdered and now I know why," Mrs. Hartman said.

"I am not saying I fully believe what happened, but why was it that only certain people saw Sarah's spirit?" Jim asked.

"I am by far not an expert on the subject," Helen offered. "But there is someone who is, and she will be in town tomorrow. Perhaps you could stop by and ask that question of her when she meets with us."

"I may just do that," Jim said. "Call or text me when your expert is available."

"Well folks, we're going to call it a night and head back to our motorhome," Hank said. "We have to meet with Sheriff Berry in the morning to give him a briefing on our investigation that I'm sure will raise a few eyebrows."

"I can't wait!" Maggie said. "I'll see you there."

"Goodnight everyone," Helen said as she and Hank turned and left.

"What a night!" Helen exclaimed as she entered the Bounder. "This was supposed to be a relaxing RV trip to Charleston to see some fireworks."

"Well, we did see some fireworks," Hank said.

Helen stopped at the kitchen sink for a glass of water and noticed the distelfink charm was hanging in the window above the sink. "Hank, the last time I saw the distelfink it was hanging in the window above the dinette and now it's back over here where it belongs! Did you move it!?"

"I didn't move it," Hank replied. "I know better than to touch your distelfink. Maybe our client gave us a message of approval for solving her case. It's always nice to receive positive feedback in one's work," Hank added laughingly.

"Well, we may find out that you're correct when Betty Hamilton arrives tomorrow," Helen responded light-heartedly.

Chapter 16

Saturday, July 5

Hank called the sheriff's office early and set up the appointment with Sheriff Berry for ten am. They arrived five minutes before the hour and Sheriff Berry escorted them into the station's conference room. In addition to Sheriff Berry, others present in the conference room were Deputy Maggie Kershaw and retired Sheriff Jim Rainey.

Sheriff Berry started the proceedings; "After his arrest last evening Brad Culpepper confessed to the murder of Sarah Payne. On behalf of the people of Thomas County, I wish to convey the counties gratitude to Mr. and Mrs. Hank Moran of Moran Investigations for taking on the cold case of the Sarah Payne murder and for finding the person responsible. It is still somewhat of a mystery as to how the Moran's, being from Louisiana, became involved in the case and who their client is that hired their agency. So, Mr. and Mrs. Moran if you would, please enlighten us as to your involvement, and present us with a summary of your investigation. For the record, this session is being recorded. Mr. and Mrs. Moran, please proceed."

Hank began; "Thank you, Sheriff Berry, for your kind words of gratitude and for your tolerance in letting us pursue this case. I'd also like to thank former Sheriff Jim Rainey for his aid and support."

"Don't forget the help and support of Mrs. Hartman at the campground for copies of the campground logs that aided in pointing out the suspect," Helen added. "We also need to praise her grandson, Eddie Parks, who had the courage to come forth as a witness to the crime."

"With all of that said we will begin the strange tale of how we became involved in the case. We were on an RV trip to Charleston when we stopped for an overnight stay at the Ochlocknee campground on Sunday, June twenty-ninth. One small strange thing happened the following morning. I'll let Helen tell you about that."

Helen related, "When I entered the kitchen to start the coffee maker I noticed the small Pennsylvania Dutch good luck charm called a distelfink I acquired on a previous road trip was missing from the window above the sink. We found that it had been moved to the window on the opposite side of our motorhome. After a brief spat about which one of us moved the charm, we had breakfast and proceeded on our way to the next planned stop in our trip which was Jesup, Georgia." Helen nodded at Hank for him to proceed.

"We arrived in Jesup on Monday, the thirtieth of June and had an uneventful afternoon. However that evening we both felt a strange chill in the motorhome. We thought the setting on the thermostat might have been changed but it was still set correctly. I'll let Helen tell you of the strange events which took place the next morning."

"Once again I intended to go out to the kitchen to start the coffee maker but as I approached the kitchen I saw a teenaged girl in the forward cabin of the motorhome. I immediately yelled for Hank and ran back to the bedroom. We then both proceeded to the forward cabin and found no one. Hank checked and found the entry door was still locked from the inside and that no one could have entered our motorhome. We had both noticed the same chill in the forward cabin. Additionally, I noticed the distelfink was once again hanging in the opposite window." Helen again nodded to Hank to continue.

"That same morning I went to the campground office to buy a newspaper and was joking with Harriet, the campground clerk, about the strange happenings in our motorhome. She laughingly said that it sounded like we had a wayward spirit traveling with us. Back at our campsite, I mentioned to Helen what Harriet had said and Helen immediately left for the campground office to talk with Harriet. I'll let her relate what happened next."

"After I arrived at the campground office I had a conversation about a possible spirit in our motorhome with Harriet the clerk which was overheard by an elderly lady also in the office. The lady named Mrs. Wright gave me a phone number of a psychic medium by the name of Betty Hamilton who lived in Jesup. I phoned Ms. Hamilton and she agreed to come out to the campground to inspect our motorhome. During Ms. Hamilton's visit, she did connect with the spirit of a young girl named Sarah. Sarah told her that she had been murdered at the Ochlocknee campground and did not actually see the suspect because she was attacked from behind and rendered unconscious. Sarah also told her that we were camped in site 22, which was the same site she and her parents had occupied when she was murdered. She noticed the Moran Investigations sign on our motorhome and decided to try to get us to investigate her murder. She wanted the case solved to provide closure for her parents before she went to the other side."

"That is quite a tale, Mrs. Moran. Are you trying to tell us that your mysterious client is the dead girl herself?" Sheriff Berry interrupted.

"I know it's hard to believe Sheriff, but what Helen has related is exactly what happened," Hank replied. "I was very skeptical myself in the beginning but there is no other explanation for what happened. We had no prior knowledge of the case and everything that Ms. Hamilton told us about the girl proved one hundred percent correct."

Both Jim Rainey and Deputy Kershaw had no comments regarding the story.

"Please proceed with your account Mr. Moran," Sheriff Berry requested.

"We arrived back in Ochlocknee Tuesday afternoon and commenced our investigation. We were able to attain the assistance of former Sheriff Rainey who provided us with his copy of the original case file. Upon questioning multiple persons and band members we uncovered the fact that there was indeed a witness to the crime, that witness being Eddie Parks, Mrs. Hartman's grandson. The rest is as we stated in the briefing we gave you yesterday. I am sure Deputy Kershaw has fully documented in her report, last evenings events that led to the apprehension of Brad Culpepper."

"Alright, Mr. and Mrs. Moran thank you for your report," Sheriff Berry said. "I too am fighting a state of skepticism of your report but as a good philosopher once said, 'Live and learn.'"

Jim Rainey uttered, "Amen," and Deputy Kershaw chuckled and said, "I'll second that!"

"So, will you be leaving us now that the case has been solved?" Sheriff Berry asked the Moran's.

"Not quite yet Sheriff," Helen replied. "Ms. Hamilton will be in town this afternoon and she wants to visit the campground to see if she can make further contact with Sarah."

"Helen, don't forget to call me when you know what time Ms. Hamilton will be at the campground," Jim Rainey requested.

"Give me a call too," Deputy Kershaw said, "I wouldn't want to miss meeting Ms. Hamilton."

"Helen chuckled and said, "I will be sure to call you both."

And with a great smile added, "Perhaps we can set up a conference call with Sarah."

Hank and Helen arrived back at their motorhome by noon.

Hank was busy grilling hamburgers out on the patio on a small electric grille when Helen received the call from Betty Hamilton.

"Hello Betty, are you in town?"

"Yes my daughter Chelsea and I arrived at my Aunts place at eleven this morning,' Betty replied.

"What time do you think you can be here at the campground," Helen asked.

"Is two o'clock okay with you," Betty replied.

"Two sounds just fine Betty. When you arrive I will have to update you on what happened last night with the apprehension of the suspect Brad Culpepper. I am sure you will find it very interesting. Also, there are two other people who requested to be present when you try to contact Sarah. One is Sheriff's Deputy Maggie Kershaw, and the other person is retired sheriff Jim Rainey. Jim Rainey was the Sheriff eleven years ago when Sarah was murdered. And Deputy Kershaw made the arrest of Culpepper last night."

"Sounds like a fascinating afternoon Helen, see you at two."

"Okay, we'll be at our motorhome in site twenty-two," Helen replied.

After disconnecting from Betty Hamilton, Helen called Jim Rainey and Deputy Kershaw and advised them of the planned meeting time with the psychic.

Two minutes later Hank received a call from Sheriff Berry.

"Good afternoon Hank, I have some news for you," Berry said.

"I hope it's all good," Hank replied jovially.

"I think you will see it that way, Hank. I just got off the phone from Mr. and Mrs. Payne. I called to inform them of the apprehension of a suspect in their daughter's murder. I informed them of your agency's successful involvement in the case and they wanted to know how you happened to be concerned with it. I thought it best not to reveal to them the high strangeness, so to speak, of your involvement, so I told them it would be best if they talk with you and Mrs. Moran. They replied that they would like to drive down tomorrow to meet you and show their appreciation. I am to call them back if you agreed to meet with them."

Hank had put the call on his phone's speaker so Helen could hear the conversation and she vigorously nodded her head yes.

"We would be happy to meet with the Paynes," Hank replied. "Give them mine and Helen's number so they can call us when they arrive in town."

"I will do that Hank and Thanks again."

After the call from Sheriff Berry, Hank rescued the burgers from the grille in the nick of time before they were overcooked. They enjoyed the burgers and sides of coleslaw and potato salad which Helen had picked up at a deli on the way back from the sheriff's office. While they were eating their lunch Helen noticed Harry and Wilma Schultz sitting out on their patio across the drive. She waved to them and they waved back.

"I have a feeling we are going to be paid a visit from Harry and Wilma when we're done eating," Helen said.

"Word probably got around the campground about last night's activities," Hank responded.

Helen glanced over across the drive and said, "Well I was right. Here they come."

Harry and Wilma approached the Moran's patio and Wilma said, "Hello Mr. and Mrs. Moran, do you have a minute?"

"Sure, come on over and have a seat. And don't be so formal. Call us Helen and Hank," Helen replied. "Now what's on your mind, Wilma?"

"Well, there is lots of talk around the campground about the arrest last night of the man that killed that girl. Everyone is saying the killer was a nephew of the fireworks man that lived nearby back behind the campground. Is that true?" Wilma enquired.

"That is only partially true Wilma," Helen replied. "Mr. Higgins, the fireworks vendor, has two nephews. One of them named Jake Higgins does live nearby the campground and the other one named Brad Culpepper lives up in Moultrie. Brad Culpepper from up in Moultrie was the one who was arrested. Jake Higgins who lives nearby is a fine young man and a war veteran."

"I see," Wilma replied. "I'm relieved we didn't have a killer living nearby. We also heard that the killer saw the dead girl's ghost last night and gave himself up. Is that true?"

"We're not exactly sure what Mr. Culpepper saw that made him put his gun down but Eddie Parks did a brave thing in kicking the gun from his hand and Sheriff's Deputy Maggie Kershaw bravely subdued the suspect and arrested him," Helen elucidated.

"Weren't you there and saw the ghost?" Wilma further enquired.

"Well, my husband and I were there, but things happened so fast that we are not exactly sure what we saw," Helen replied.

"Well okay, we just wanted to see if the rumors were correct," Wilma said.

Harry and Wilma walked back across the driveway and sat once again on their patio. Their next-door neighbors immediately joined them to catch the latest gossip.

"I guess I was a little evasive with Wilma but I didn't want to expound too much about the presence of Sarah's spirit especially with Betty Hamilton arriving soon," Helen explained. "I don't want to take any chances in having a big audience when Betty does her thing."

"I guess you're right," Hank said. "The audience will be big enough with us, Jim Rainey, and Deputy Kershaw."

Chapter 17

Betty Hamilton and her fourteen-year-old daughter Chelsea arrived right on time at two. Hank and Helen were waiting on the patio and greeted them on their arrival.

"Hello Betty, I'm so glad you could make it," Helen greeted.

"It's my pleasure," Betty replied. "I want you to meet my daughter Chelsea."

Hank and Helen greeted Chelsea with a handshake. When Chelsea shook Helen's hand the teenaged girl said, "You can feel things, Mrs. Moran."

"Chelsea shares some of the abilities I had at her age," Betty explained. "I am hoping Sarah's spirit will be even more inclined to commune with another young girl."

"Okay, let's go inside and I'll explain what happened last night," Helen said.

Upon entering the Moran's motorhome, Betty paused and said, "Sarah's spirit is no longer here in your RV, but I sense she is in the area."

"She is down by the water," Chelsea said matter-of-factly. "That is where she was hurt."

"Yes, you are right," Helen said. "After I tell you and your mother what happened last night, we can all walk down to the lake and you can try to talk with her."

Helen related last night's events to the couple about Culpepper holding his cousin Jake and Eddie Parks at gunpoint and about the ensuing standoff with Deputy Kershaw. Chelsea smiled when Helen told them how Sarah's spirit appeared and had a direct effect on Culpepper, making his arrest possible by Deputy Kershaw.

"Sarah liked Eddie. She didn't want the man to hurt him," Chelsea offered.

"Are you in contact with Sarah now?" Betty asked her daughter.

"A little bit, she wants us to go down to the lake," Chelsea replied.

"Oh, I almost forgot to tell you that Sarah's parents will be in town tomorrow to meet Hank and I. I think you should mention it to Sarah," Helen said.

"Yes you are right, Sarah would want to know," Betty replied.

At that moment there was a knock on the door. Hank greeted Jim Rainey and Deputy Maggie Kershaw and invited them in.

"I'm sorry we're a little late. I had to handle a small fender bender over on Rt. 188 first," Maggie explained.

"It's no problem," Helen said. "We just finished telling Ms. Hamilton and her daughter Chelsea about last night."

Helen introduced Betty and her daughter to Jim Rainey and Deputy Kershaw. "Now that we all know each other, let's not be so formal. First names only please," Helen insisted.

"Chelsea said that Sarah wants us to go down to the lake," Helen added.

"Oh my Chelsea, do you have the same abilities as your mother?" Maggie asked.

"Yeah some, my mom is better though," Chelsea replied.

Betty laughed and said, "Chelsea is being a little modest. She has more abilities than I had at her age."

"I still find it a little scary," Chelsea said and then added, "Sarah is waiting for us down at the lake. We better go!"

Harry and Wilma Schultz were sitting out on their patio when the group exited the Moran's motorhome. Helen and Hank waved to them and then led the entourage towards the lake. "I wonder what they are up to," Wilma remarked.

As the group neared the lake Betty said, "Chelsea and I need to stand near the spot where Sarah died."

Jim pointed and said, "Her body was found just on the other side of that small bridge."

"Right where the rock is," Chelsea remarked.

"You're right Chelsea," Jim said.

The group reached the bridge and Betty said, "I think it's best if y'all wait here while Chelsea and I go on over the bridge."

After Betty and her daughter walked over the bridge Jim Rainey said, "I wonder how Chelsea knew about the rock? Did you mention it to them, Helen?"

"I am sure they only knew that Sarah was murdered here in the campground. I never told Betty about how it happened or even when it happened for that matter," Helen replied.

"Then how did Chelsea know?" Jim asked again.

"Could it be she's psychic?" Helen replied with a smile chiding Jim.

Hank, Helen, Jim, and Maggie watched Betty and Chelsea seemingly converse with some unseen entity on the other side of the bridge. It appeared to the four of them that Chelsea did most of the conversing. After about ten minutes Betty and Chelsea returned to the group.

"We were successful in contacting Sarah," Betty said and added. "Helen, why don't we go back to your motorhome and Chelsea and I will fill you in on what Sarah told us? I think it's best if we go somewhere private because there were a number of spirits that contacted us."

As the group approached the motorhome Wilma again waved from across the drive and spoke softly to Harry,

"That's the sheriff's deputy that was here last night and also that is the old sheriff. I wonder why they took a walk down to the lake?"

"You're just too nosey Wilma," Harry replied.

"Oh hush yourself," Wilma retorted.

The group entered the motorhome and Helen, Maggie, Jim, and Hank found seats as Betty and Chelsea stood before them.

"As I mentioned when we were down at the lake, we were able to commune with Sarah," Betty began. "She said she is very grateful to all of you for finding the person who attacked her. She is hoping her parents will now be able to find closure. I also told Sarah her parents are coming down to the campground tomorrow and she requested that Chelsea and I meet with them down by the lake. She said there are relatives waiting to accompany her to the other side but she wants to tell her parents something before she leaves.

"As I also mentioned before there were some other spirits that contacted us down by the lake. Helen, your mother Abigail said she is proud of you and also amused that you have become a private detective. She said you always had a very inquisitive mind. She also mentioned she was in the cornfield with you."

"Oh my!" Helen exclaimed. "A few years ago I had to hide in a cornfield up in Michigan to escape from some crazy militia group that abducted me. I remember feeling safe and secure in that cornfield as if someone had put their arms around me. I recalled it was the same feeling I got when my mother hugged me when I was a little girl."

"She also said she would not have let the dog harm you," Betty added.

Helen chuckled and said, "When I left the cornfield and walked to a neighboring farm there was a large watchdog that growled viciously at me. I thought I had sweet-talked the dog into being friendly, but I guess it was my mom's doing. It's comforting to know she is still watching over me, thank you, Betty."

Chelsea turned to Deputy Kershaw and said, "Maggie, Billy said to tell you this; "For Pete's sake Mags it's been five years and it's time to move on and let someone else into your heart."

Maggie stood there teary-eyed and said, "My husband Billy always called me Mags and he always started out by saying "For Pete's Sake Mags" whenever he disagreed with me. He was killed in Iraq five years ago. I loved him so much that I thought I could never love some else again without feeling a pang of guilt. There is someone else who has feelings for me but I always have the excuse that I'm not ready for a new relationship. Now, knowing that he wants me to move on I will be open to letting someone else into my heart. Thank you, Chelsea."

"Jim and Hank," Betty began, "Your spirit guides said they are around you but that you both have a problem of recognizing when they are trying to help you."

"What the heck is a spirit guide?" asked Hank.

Betty went on to explain; "Whenever someone from the other side decides to enter into a new physical life on this side, an arrangement is made with another spirit to guide that spirit throughout his or her physical life to attain the goals that spirit desired to achieve."

"So you are saying that my spirit is trying to reach some lofty goal?" Hank asked.

"It doesn't have to be a lofty goal," Betty replied. "It could simply be a goal to help others or just to be a better person. It is usually something that was lacking in a previous life and needs to be tweaked a little."

"Well, how would I know when my spirit guide is trying to tell me something?" Hank asked.

"Sometimes you might get a message in a dream or something more subtle that you might attribute to your intuition," Betty replied. "Also a good thing to remember is that sometimes a coincidence might not be a coincidence at all. There might be a message hidden in there."

Jim Rainey sat listening intently to the conversation between Betty and Hank and then asked; "Ms. Betty, in line with what you were telling Hank, is it possible that the appearance of Hank and Helen in my life and their help to solve the Sarah Payne case might not be a coincidence? It was a case that I desperately wanted to be solved before I left this earth."

"Jim, I know you may find this hard to believe but I did get the impression from Sarah that her and your guides played a part in guiding Sarah to seek the aid of Hank and Helen."

"Well doesn't that beat all?" Jim replied. "I can't wait to tell my wife Flo about this. She's a big believer in things of this nature."

"Okay, I think Chelsea and I covered all the bases today so we'll be heading back to my aunt's place," Betty concluded. "Helen, call me when you find out what time Mr. and Mrs. Payne want to meet with you. Sarah wants me to accompany them down to the lake."

"I wouldn't know how to even begin to explain to Mr. and Mrs. Payne all that happened with Sarah's spirit without you helping me. So if at all possible could you be here when they arrive?

"You bet I can. Call me," Betty replied.

Chapter 18

Sunday, July 6

Hank and Helen had spent a restful night in the Bounder with no sudden cold spots. Just the normal cool air from the rooftop air conditioner trying to keep a hot July night in Georgia at bay.

The next morning when Helen went into the kitchen to start the coffee maker she smiled when she saw the distelfink hanging in the window above the sink where it belonged.

Hank came out of the bedroom dresses in a polo shirt and jogging shorts and noticed Helen's smile. "You look happy this morning," He said to his wife.

"I came out to the kitchen this morning and my distelfink wasn't moved overnight. It's right where it belongs. No mischievous spirits."

"I guess our client is happy with us then," Hank replied.

I'm going to take a run around the campground and pick up a Sunday paper over at the office."

"Okay, I'll have breakfast ready in twenty minutes," Helen replied.

Hank returned from his run with the leftover Saturday edition of the *Thomasville Times-Enterprise* and the Sunday edition of the *Albany Herald*. They enjoyed a breakfast of fried hash browns, scrambled eggs, and sausage links. After breakfast, Helen sought a comfortable seat on the sofa to work on the Sunday crossword while Hank checked the news for reports of the arrest of Brad Culpepper.

The Saturday edition of the Thomasville paper had a headline which read; "Eleven-Year-old Campground Murder Solved." The ensuing article gave a brief history of the case and details of the Friday night apprehension of Culpepper. Apparently, the sheriff's department was keeping mum about any spirits involved as there was no mention of any unnatural aspects of the arrest. Credit for the arrest was given to Deputy Kershaw and the Moran Investigations agency was given credit for uncovering information that led to Culpepper as the suspect. Hank noticed the article was written by Jason Hicks who was also the reporter who covered the case eleven years ago.

"Hey, partner! We made the newspaper," Hank said when he finished reading the article.

"Any mention of Sarah's appearance?" Helen asked.

"No, not at all," Hank replied. "It appears the sheriff's department didn't want to broach the subject."

"Who was Giants pitcher Maglie, three letters?" Helen asked needing a solution to her crossword puzzle.

"Sal," Hank replied. "Guess who wrote the article on Culpepper's arrest?"

"The same reporter as eleven years ago?" Helen asked.

"You're right partner, Jason Hicks," Hank replied. "I wonder if he'll be doing a follow-up article for Monday's edition."

"I have a feeling that he'll soon track us down for an interview," Helen said as there was a knock on the Bounder's door.

Hank arose and opened the door to see a thin middle-aged man wearing a brown porkpie hat with a small feather stuck in the brim. "Hello, can I help you?" Hank inquired.

"Hello sir, I'm Jason Hicks from the *Thomasville Times-Enterprise*. Are you Mr. Moran of Moran Investigations?"

"Yes, I am Hank Moran. What brings you out here on this fine Sunday morning Mr. Hicks?"

"I want to do a follow-up story on the Sarah Payne case and Sheriff Berry said your agency was heavily involved in solving the case. I researched your agency online and found that you are based in Louisiana. I think our readers would be interested to know how you became involved in a case so far from home."

"Okay Mr. Hicks, have a seat at the picnic table and my wife and I will be right out."

Hank closed the door and turned to Helen and said, "Well, you said you had a feeling that Jason Hicks was going to track us down. He's waiting outside. I guess Chelsea was right when she told you that you can feel things."

"Don't get overly excited big guy," Helen replied. "I saw him through the front window when he walked up. I just guessed that someone wearing a porkpie hat with a feather in it looked like a newspaper reporter."

"Brilliant deduction, Watson!" Hank said. "C'mon, I guess we have to go out and talk to him."

Hank introduced Helen to Jason Hicks as his wife and agency partner.

"It's a pleasure to meet you, Mrs. Moran," Hicks said when he shook hands with Helen and then went right into the questions. "Okay, my first question is; how did your agency become involved in the case?"

Hank replied, "We were taking time off from our agency work for an RV trip to Charleston when we stopped for an overnight stay here at the campground. We heard talk about an unsolved murder that occurred here back in o-three and it piqued our interest."

"So you stayed and decided to investigate?" Hicks asked.

"Well no, not exactly," Helen replied. "We continued our trip the next morning and stopped at a campground up in Jessup before heading over to Charleston. We kept thinking about the unsolved case back in Thomasville and being investigators we decided to head back there the next morning to look into the case."

"I see. How did retired sheriff Rainey get involved in your investigation?" Hicks continued.

"We found out the sheriff at the time of the murder was now retired and we contacted him to obtain background information," Hank replied. "It just so happened that Ex-Sheriff Rainey had made a copy of his case file with the intent of continuing the investigation after he retired. He let us borrow his file in order to bring us up to speed on the case and he agreed to help us in any way he could."

"What was the one thing you uncovered, that Sheriff Rainey wasn't able to eleven years ago, that broke the case?"

"Through questioning multiple people we discovered there was a witness to the crime who didn't come forward at the time for fear of bodily harm," Helen replied.

"Hmm, who was the witness?" Hicks inquired.

"Didn't Sheriff Berry provide that information?" Hank asked with a wrinkled brow and a stare at Hicks.

"I asked him but Sheriff Berry refused to volunteer the identity of the witness pending Culpepper's trial," Hicks responded.

"Then I don't think it's proper for us to say or do anything contrary to Sheriff Berry's wishes," Hank replied. "I think we are done here, Mr. Hicks."

"Just one more question Mr. Moran; did you investigate the case for the reward?" Hicks probed.

"What reward are you talking about?" Hank asked brusquely.

"One month after their daughter's murder the Paynes offered a ten thousand dollar reward to anyone with information that led directly to the arrest of their daughter's killer," Hicks replied. "It was in the newspaper."

"We knew nothing about the reward," Hank replied.

Hicks momentarily thought about asking further questions but because of the scowl on Hank's face, he thanked them for their time and walked back up toward the campground office where he had parked.

"I guess we should have checked a few more weeks of the newspaper down at the library. We would have seen the article about the reward," Hank said.

When Hicks was out of earshot Helen remarked, "I'm glad Sheriff Berry decided to keep Eddie out of the news. I am sure his gramma wouldn't want him talking to a reporter."

"I am sure the sheriff had his reasons," Hank replied. "Foremost of which would be some denigrating news article of the witness by an overzealous reporter that Culpepper's defense could use in the trial."

"I see what you mean," Helen replied. "I hope Eddie's mother is coming to pick him up today to take him home. Do you think we should talk with Mrs. Hartman about it?"

"It wouldn't be a bad idea," Hank replied.

Hank and Helen walked by the campground office on the way to Mrs. Hartmann's cottage and noticed there were no cars in the parking lot. "It looks like Hicks is gone," Helen said as they stepped up onto Mrs. Hartman's front porch and knocked on the door. They heard footsteps running toward the door and when it opened Eddie greeted them with a big smile and said, "Hello Mr. and Mrs. Moran." Eddie proceeded to give Helen a short hug.

"Who is it Eddie?" came Mrs. Hartman's voice from a back room.

"It's the detectives," Eddie shouted back.

After Mrs. Hartman greeted them, Hank and Helen explained the purpose of their visit and to caution Mrs.

Hartman about letting Eddie be interviewed by any news people.

"I understand completely," Mrs. Hartman said. "And thank you for rescuing Eddie Friday night. He told me what happened and how Culpepper saw the girl and was frightened and put his weapon down."

"Yes it was a strange night all around," Helen said.

"I saw the girl too!" Eddie said after hearing the previous conversation.

"I am sure you did Eddie, but you must keep it a secret for a little while. Can you do that? Helen asked.

Eddie then made the gesture of zipping his mouth closed and Helen chuckled and gave him a hug.

"My daughter is due here this afternoon to take Eddie back home," Mrs. Hartman said. "This will be a Fourth of July weekend he'll never forget."

As Hank and Helen were walking back to their campsite Hanks cell phone chimed with a call from Sheriff Berry.

"Good morning Sheriff, this is Hank."

"Hank, I just wanted to let you know that the Paynes just called and they should be in the area just after noon. They will be going directly to the campground. They have your number and will call you when they arrive."

"Thanks for the heads-up Sheriff. We're looking forward to meeting them."

After the call from Sheriff Berry, Helen called Betty Hamilton and arranged for her and Chelsea to come to the campground at noon. Helen was grateful to have Betty present to help with the disclosure that their daughter's spirit still remained at the campground.

Hank called Jim Rainey to inform him of the Payne's planned visit and to invite him to participate in the meeting. Jim declined the meeting stating he had to accompany his wife to an afternoon church bazaar.

"I'm kind of glad Jim isn't coming to the meeting with the Paynes," Helen said. "I think it should be kept as private as possible not knowing how the Paynes will react to the news about Sarah's lingering spirit."

"I agree," replied Hank. "When I was on the force I had to inform a number of families about the death of a loved one and their reaction of grief was always predictable. But this is totally different. The Payne's initial period of grief is long past. The arrest of Culpepper should bring some closure. I have no idea how the knowledge of Sarah's spirit lingering here at the campground will play out."

"Well I'm hoping that Betty will be able to explain the situation to them in a believable way," Helen replied.

Chapter 19

Betty Hamilton knocked on the Bounder's door at precisely twelve noon. Helen invited Betty and Chelsea into the Bounder and gave them both hugs. Hank emerged from the rear bedroom, freshly showered, wearing tan cargo pants and a navy blue polo shirt. Hank greeted Betty and Chelsea with a handshake.

"What do you think is the best way to approach the subject of Sarah's spirit to the Paynes," Helen asked Betty.

"I assume they are coming to visit to thank you for finding their daughter's murderer. When they ask you how you became involved in the case I suggest that you start from the beginning of your trip and tell the story exactly how it happened. I am sure they will be unbelieving at first but when they hear about Sarah's wishes they might become more receptive."

"I agree with you Betty," Hank added. "And we should just ease into the story to make it more palatable a small piece at a time. I know I was skeptical at first but now I accept all that happened as fact."

Helen's cell phone chimed and she recognized the Paynes number she had received from Sheriff Berry. "Hello, this is Helen Moran speaking."

"Mrs. Moran, this is Carol Payne. We just parked up at the campground office. We'll walk to your campsite from here."

"We're looking forward to meeting you, Mrs. Payne. We are in site twenty-two in the black and gold Bounder."

There was a momentary period of silence, and then Carol Payne said, "I'm sure we can find your site," and ended the call.

"It sounded like Mrs. Payne was taken aback when I mentioned we were in site twenty-two. Maybe we should have moved to another site before their visit," Helen said.

"It will be all right," Betty replied. "I am sure their bad memories starting flowing as soon as they entered the campground."

Two minutes later there was a knock on the Bounder door. Hank greeted the late middle-aged couple, Greg and Carol Payne, and invited them into the motorhome. Introductions were made all around but the reason for Betty's and Chelsea's presence was not divulged at this time. In the ensuing conversation it was learned that Greg Payne is a professor of economics at the University of Georgia and Carol Payne is a Guidance Counselor at the same. Betty introduced herself as a paralegal in a law office in Jessup and Chelsea a student at Jessup junior High School. Hank described his background of thirty years' service on the Kenner, Louisiana police force and after retiring became a private investigator and opened the Moran Investigations Agency along with Helen who also is a licensed PI.

After all, formalities were dispensed with Greg Payne said, "Well Hank, the purpose of our visit is to thank you and Helen for finding Sarah's killer. We are also very curious as to how you became involved in the case."

"Greg we are going to tell you a story that you and Carol may find unbelievable and also hard to accept. But we are going to tell it exactly as it happened and then you can make up your own minds," Hank replied. "We started out on an RV trip to Charleston with this campground being our first stop. When we awoke in the morning Helen noticed something amiss in the kitchen." Hank nodded to Helen to proceed.

"I have a Pennsylvania Dutch good look charm called a distelfink that I acquired up in Lancaster Pennsylvania. I keep it hanging in the window above the kitchen sink. However that first morning it was missing and later found hanging in the window above the dinette. A cold chill was also felt in the motorhome. We left that morning for our second stop up in Jessup. While in the Jessup campground I saw an image of a teenaged girl in the front of the motorhome. There was also another cold chill in the air and once again the distelfink was relocated. In talking with some people in the campground office it was mentioned that we might have picked up a spirit back at this campground. We learned of a medium named Betty Hamilton, who lived in Jessup, that an elderly lady at the campground said might be able to help us. We contacted Betty and she agreed to check our motorhome."

"Carol Payne turned to Betty and asked, "You are a medium?"

"Yes, I am, Carol. It is a gift I became aware of as a young child. My daughter Chelsea also has the gift."

"Betty, why don't you tell Carol and Greg what happened when you came to our motorhome," Helen asked.

"After Helen explained to me what happened in their motorhome and her seeing an apparition, I entered the motorhome to see if I could contact any possible spirits. I successfully made contact with a teenaged girl named Sarah who was murdered back at this campground. She saw the Moran Investigations sign on the Moran's motorhome and decided to seek their help in finding her murderer. She said that she was attacked from behind and did not actually see her attacker. She also said she wanted to bring closure for her parents."

When Betty was finished Helen continued, "After hearing Betty's report Hank and I decided to return here to

Thomasville to seek further information on the murder. When we arrived back here we learned from the campground owner, Mrs. Hartman, that there was indeed a murder of a girl named Sarah Payne here at the campground back in two thousand and three and the murderer was never found. It was at that point we decided to take Sarah on as our client so to speak. Hank, why don't you tell of our investigation?"

"We contacted retired sheriff Jim Rainey for his background information on the case and as it turned out Sarah's case was still troubling him after seven years into retirement. Before he left the office he made a complete copy of the case file in order to continue his investigation. He let us borrow the file and proceeded to aid us in our investigation. Upon questioning the locals we uncovered the fact that there was an actual witness to the crime who was threatened with bodily harm by the murderer to keep quiet about what he saw. That witness was Mrs. Hartman's grandson, Eddie Parks, who has Down syndrome. Eddie identified the assailant on a campground photograph that was taken at the time. The photograph was hanging in the campground office. The fourth of July fireworks vendor, Joe Higgins, identified the person pointed out in the picture by Eddie Parks as Higgins nephew Brad Culpepper. Culpepper was arrested Friday night at his cousin's house. His cousin Jake Higgins lives about a quarter of a mile behind the campground. Unknown to us Eddie had gone to Jakes house to check on him when we were unable to contact Jake on his cell phone. I'll let Helen explain the rest."

"Eddie had left a note at his grandmother's house saying he went to check on Jake. Suspecting that something was amiss at Jake's house, Hank, Joe Higgins, Deputy Sheriff Maggie Kershaw, and I, went to Jakes house to investigate. Hank crept to a window and saw Culpepper holding a gun on Jake and Eddie. Hank snuck in the back door and Deputy Kershaw and I entered the house through the front door. Next, there was a standoff at gunpoint with Culpepper holding a gun to Eddie's head. Suddenly an apparition of Sarah appeared in front of Deputy Kershaw and me. Culpepper was visibly awe-stricken by the apparition, blurted out "It's her," released Eddie and lowered his weapon. Eddie then kicked the gun out of Culpepper's hand, Hank forced Culpepper to the floor, and Deputy Kershaw Cuffed him."

Greg and Carol Payne sat mesmerized by the story then Carol asked in a low voice, "Did everyone in the house see Sarah's apparition at the time of the arrest?"

"I believe the only ones present who saw her was me, Culpepper, and Eddie Parks, Helen replied.

"Why is it that only certain people saw her?" Greg Payne asked with a hint of suspicion.

"Let me answer that," Betty offered. "Some people have the ability to see those that have passed over, but more often than not the spirit will be visible to only those that the spirit desires. In other words, a spirit can pick and choose who to be visible to. In Helen's case, Sarah chose to be visible to her to further the chance that Helen would begin the investigation. Eddie Parks, on the other hand, has the ability to see the departed. It is just second nature to him and he thinks it isn't anything special. Chelsea was drawn to have a brief chat with him yesterday before we left the campground."

"How do we know this isn't just some sort of scam?" Greg Payne brusquely asked.

"Greg, can't you see these people are only trying to help!" Carol Payne said admonishing her husband.

"Greg, I assure you, we are not trying to pull some sort of scam as we have nothing to gain by it," Hank added. "What we told you is the absolute truth. Neither Helen and I nor Betty Hamilton knew anything of this case before we arrived here in Thomasville. I can appreciate you being skeptical as was I in the beginning. But those are the facts and we stand by them."

"It's just so hard to believe that our daughter's spirit was hanging around this campground just waiting for someone to solve her murder," Greg said. "It's been eleven years since her death for God's sake."

"Mr. Payne, from what I have learned in my experience a spirit such as Sarah's has no awareness of time," Betty said. "For her time is nonexistent. It would be like her death only happened yesterday."

"Betty, you mentioned earlier that Sarah wanted her murderer found to bring closure for us, so what happens now that the case is solved?" Carol Payne asked.

"Yesterday Chelsea and I were able to contact Sarah down by the lake," Betty replied. "She stated that she is now ready to complete her journey to the other side. She has guides and relatives waiting to help her on her journey. The journey and her acclimation on the other side could be a little difficult since she spent an extended period on this side. She requested that Chelsea and I accompany you and Mr. Payne

Down to the lake as she has some things to tell you before she departs."

"How will she communicate with us?" Carol asked.

"That is the purpose of mediums such as Chelsea and I," Betty answered. "We will receive the messages from Sarah and relay them to you. She will be able to hear your response."

"How will we know that we are actually communicating with our daughter?" Greg Payne asked again being skeptical.

"Don't worry Mr. Payne; I am sure Sarah will come up with something only you or Mrs. Payne and nobody else can verify," Betty replied.

"Mr. Payne your father Ben said you should stop being such a hard head," Chelsea said. "He said he sees you still haven't grown out of that."

Greg Payne looked at Chelsea as if in shock and Carol Payne said, "Your dad always did call you a hard head, Greg. Maybe now you can lose your skepticism."

Greg just uttered something unintelligible and then asked, "Are you trying to tell me that you just talked to my father?"

"Of course," Chelsea said. "He was right behind you but he's gone now. Before he left he said you still have to work on your ten-foot putts."

Greg Payne looked stunned, "Now that you could NOT have known! Whenever we played golf together we always had a little putting contest before each round. He always beat me on the ten-foot putts."

"Now I think we are ready for a walk down to the lake," Carol Payne said with a smile.

Chapter 20

Hank and Helen led the way down the well-worn path to the lake. Greg and Carol Payne followed next with Betty and Chelsea walking behind. As they approached the bridge that crossed the small feeder stream they saw Eddie Parks standing on the middle of it. He was smiling and seemed transfixed on a spot twenty feet away on the near side of the lake. Chelsea called for everyone to please stop for a minute.

After about thirty seconds Eddie became aware of the group and turned to them and said hi.

"Hi Eddie," Chelsea said returning the greeting.

"I came down to say goodbye to the girl," Eddie said.

"We came to say goodbye also," Chelsea replied. "You are welcome to stay here with us Eddie."

Eddie just replied, "Okay."

The group crossed the bridge and gathered at the spot where Sarah's body was found eleven years ago. Betty requested everyone to be quiet as she attempted to contact Sarah.

A moment later Betty said to Greg and Carol Payne, "Sarah is very happy that both of you came down to see her off on her new adventure. She also said she is happy that mom found the pair of diamond stud earrings that she had borrowed for the senior prom."

Carol Payne, with tears in her eyes, involuntarily reached up and touched her right ear which held one of the diamond studs.

Betty continued, "She wants both of you to know that while sitting here by the lake that night, she decided to accept the scholarship at the University of Georgia and not attend Yale up in Connecticut. She loves you both and she is sorry that she caused you so much trouble about the schools. She also wants you to know that Auntie Flo and Uncle Pete are with her."

"Sarah always called her great aunt Florence, Auntie Flo. Sarah was like a granddaughter she never had," Carol explained. "Sarah was devastated when Aunt Florence and Uncle Pete were killed in an auto accident fifteen years ago on Interstate 85 near Atlanta."

Betty held up her hand and squinted her eyes as if listening closely to someone and said, "Carol, Aunt Florence said you are not to worry about Sarah because she and Uncle Pete will be with her on her journey."

Betty then turned to Hank and Helen, "Sarah wants to thank you both for helping to bring closure for her mom and dad."

"You're quite welcome Sarah," Helen replied. "And you are always welcome to come along for a ride in our motorhome."

"Sarah said thank you, but she always causes too much trouble with the thermostat," Betty conveyed.

That statement by Sarah caused both Hank and Helen to chuckle.

Betty continued, "Sarah said it is now time to go. She said goodbye mom and dad and Eddie."

Carol Payne, being obviously choked up, managed to say, "Goodbye sweetheart, and listen to Auntie Flo and Uncle Pete!"

A brief moment later Eddie waved as if sending someone off on a journey and said, "She's gone now."

"Yes she is Eddie," Betty confirmed.

Out of curiosity Carol Payne asked, "Eddie, were you able to see Sarah?"

"Yes I saw her," Eddie replied.

"Why was Eddie able to see her and we weren't?" Carol asked.

"As I said before, Eddie has a special gift similar to mine and Chelsea's," Betty replied. He is able to see some spirits but is not on a level to communicate with them. Sarah chose not to be visible to you and Mr. Payne because she thought you would get too emotional if you saw her."

"I guess Sarah was correct on that point," Carol replied. "When we lost her eleven years ago I had to be hospitalized for two days. It would have been very distressing to see her once again and then seem to lose her a second time. It is comforting to know that she will be fine on the other side. She will be heaven's gain."

"Well, I believe we are finished down here unless you and Mr. Payne wish to remain for a while," Betty said.

"No, I think we are okay," Carol replied. Greg has something he wants to discuss with Hank up in their motorhome.

When the group reached the Bounder, Eddie said he had to go to his Grammas house as his mother was waiting to drive him home. Everyone said goodbye to Eddie and Helen gave him a hug. When Helen hugged him Eddie said, "You hug good Mrs. Moran."

Everyone smiled as Eddie turned and ran towards his Gramma's house.

Betty said that she and Chelsea had to hurry back to her aunt's place for a late afternoon cookout. Carol Payne gave Betty a hug and thanked her for making it possible for her to say goodbye to Sarah.

Betty said goodbye to Hank and Helen and told them that she would be in touch with them about the manuscript.

"Greg, Carol mentioned there was something you wanted to discuss with me. Shall we go into the Bounder?" Hank offered.

When the two couples were seated in the motorhome Greg spoke, "Hank, Carol and I are very appreciative of your work in finding our daughter's assailant. We feel that we should compensate you for your time and expenses. If you would send us an invoice with your normal rates we would be more than happy to write you a check. And one more thing, a few months after our daughter's death we offered a ten thousand dollar reward for anyone who would come forward with information that would bring Sarah's murderer to justice. That reward offer is still standing and we believe you and Helen have earned it."

"Greg, we learned, only this morning, about the reward you offered from a local newspaper reporter named Jason Hicks. Helen and I had a discussion about what to do with the reward if it was offered. The actual person who came forth with the information that led to solving the case was Eddie Parks and we feel it should go to him. We also feel it is unnecessary to compensate us for our time and expenses. To tell you the truth we totally enjoyed being a part of this, how should I say, very unique experience, and being monetarily compensated for it would only diminish it. It will be a road trip we will never forget."

"Well okay Hank, thanks again for all you and Helen have done and if you ever happen to get up by Athens on one of your road trips please stop in. We have an RV pad right by the house for you to park your rig in.

"We'll remember that Greg and have a safe trip back home," Hank replied.

"We better leave now and try to catch Eddie and his mother before they leave," Greg said.

Greg and Hank shook hands and Carol gave both Helen and Hank a hug and thanked them again for their help. The Paynes caught up with Eddie and his mother as they were leaving Mrs. Hartman's front porch. Greg simply asked for their home mailing address for the purpose of sending Eddie a thank you note. He didn't want to mention the reward at this time for fear that Mrs. Parks wouldn't accept it. He would explain the reward check in the thank you note they shall soon receive.

Hank and Helen had stepped outside with the Paynes when they left. Helen noticed Wilma and Harry Schultz across the drive sitting out on their patio and gave them a wave. Harry and Wilma waved back.

"It must be driving Wilma crazy watching all of the people come and go from our site today and trying to guess what all is going on," Helen said to Hank in a low tone so as to not be heard by Wilma.

"You mean you're not going over there and explain it all to her?" Hank jokingly replied.

"Heavens no!" Helen exclaimed. "She'd keep me there all night with her questions. I think I'll just write her a note and put it in her campground mailbox when we leave in the morning."

"Oh, about leaving," Hank said. "I'm not in a real hurry to head back home right away. Do you have any suggestions?"

"Funny you should ask," Helen replied. "I still have a half-full plastic casino cup of quarters I won on the slots on our last stop in Biloxi. They have a full hookup RV park at the Hollywood Casino in Bay St. Louis. I'm sure we would have no problem securing a reservation for a Monday."

"That sounds like fun," Hank replied. "I'll try to limit my losses at the blackjack table. On second thought, maybe we shouldn't have turned down the reward from the Paynes."

"Believe me; I am sure the Parks can put the reward to much better use," Helen retorted.

"You are probably right," Hank replied. "I'm a heck of a better investigator than a gambler."

"Should we get in touch with Jim Rainey and Sheriff Berry to let them know we will be leaving in the morning?" Helen asked.

"I was just about to dial Sheriff Berry when you mentioned it," Hank replied. "Chelsea did mention that you can feel things."

"Weee u weee u," Helen replied laughingly in a falsetto voice.

Hank punched in Sheriff Berry's number and he answered after five rings, "Sheriff Berry speaking."

"Hello Sheriff, this is Hank Moran, did I catch you at a bad time?"

"No Hank, not at all, just in the middle of flipping some steaks on the grill."

"I just wanted to let you know that we will be heading back to Louisiana in the morning and wanted to know if you need anything more from us."

"No Hank, thanks for asking. We have everything buttoned down tight in the Sarah Payne case. As you know, we have a confession from Culpepper and he will soon make an appearance before the judge for sentencing.

"That sounds good Sheriff. Would you please say goodbye to Deputy Kershaw for us when you get back to the station."

"She's right here, I can tell her right now, Hank."

"Oh, are you having a department cookout?" Hank asked.

"No, it's just me and her," Berry replied.

"Oh, I see. Well, I'll let you get to it then Sheriff. I wouldn't want to hold you up and have you burn those steaks. Have a nice evening Sheriff."

"I'm sure we will. Thanks for calling Hank, bye."

When the call ended, Hank called loudly to Helen who was back in the bedroom, "Hey partner, guess who Sheriff Berry is having a private cookout with."

"Maggie Kershaw," Helen shouted back.

"Huh, I should have known better than to ask," Hank said to himself.

Hank then proceeded to call Jim Rainey to tell him they will be leaving in the morning and to thank him for his help in solving Sarah Payne's murder. Jim assured Hank that all of the thanks should be directed to him and Helen. Jim said he is sleeping much better now that the case has been solved.

Chapter 21

As they were preparing to leave in the morning, Helen noticed that Harry and Wilma Schultz's Buick wasn't parked by their campsite. Helen proceeded to write them a note and instead of dropping it into their campground mailbox she walked over and stuck it in the door of their fifth wheel trailer.

As they were pulling out of the Ochlocknee campground Hank asked, "What did you say in the note to the Schultz's?"

"I just told them it was nice meeting them and if they wanted to know the true story about what happened with the Sarah Payne investigation that they should be on the lookout for a soon to be published book by an author named Betty Hamilton. And to be sure to look for a chapter entitled 'Site 22.'"

It was approximately three hundred and seventy miles to Bay St. Louis and with stopping to fuel up and a respite at a rest area on I-10; they arrived at the Hollywood Casino RV Park in the late afternoon. After taking time to rest and freshen up, they had a seafood dinner at Bogart's restaurant and then proceeded to the casino. The din of slot machine handles being pulled was like music to Helen's ears and she was drawn in that direction. Hank headed to the blackjack tables.

The tally after two hours gambling added up to; Hank minus thirty-five dollars and Helen a refilled plastic casino cup of quarters.

The remainder of the trip back to their home in Kenner was less than seventy-five miles and they arrived right at noon.

Helen was in her bedroom rehanging some clothes from the Bounder when she got the feeling she should call Mrs. Tolliver to see how she was doing with her Lhasa Apso, Twinkles. When she dialed Mrs. Tolliver's number a younger woman answered, "Hello, Suzy Abrams speaking."

"Hello Ms. Abrams, I'm Helen Moran and would like to speak with Mrs. Tolliver."

"I'm sorry, but my mother passed away last Wednesday," Suzy Abrams replied.

"Oh, I'm so sorry to hear that. I had just found her missing dog Twinkles for her the week before and the feeling just came over on me to check on her. If I may ask, what happened to her?"

"Her heart finally gave out and her neighbor found her when she heard Twinkles crying."

"Oh poor Twinkles, I bet he really misses her."

"Yes, he does. He wouldn't eat for a day or two but he is finally coming around.

"I'm sorry if I sound nosy, but what is going to happen to him," Helen asked.

"I really don't know what to do with him. My mother's funeral was yesterday and I have to get back to my work over in Montgomery. My job requires me to travel a lot and I fear that I can't take him in. I was thinking of taking him to the shelter today right before you called."

"Oh wait, I know someone who might be happy to take him," Helen replied. "Give me about an hour and I'll get back with you."

Helen hung up and hurried to the front door, "I'll be back in an hour Hank."

"Where are you going . . . ?" Hank managed to say before the front door closed with a bang and he heard the Honda's tires squeal out of the driveway.

Helen made the normal eighteen-minute drive to Caroline Hebert's house in fourteen minutes. To her dismay when she knocked on the front door she heard the bark of a small dog.

Caroline Hebert answered the door with a small brown and white dog at her side. "Mrs. Moran, to what do I owe this visit?"

"Oh, I see you have a dog. Is that the one from the shelter I told you about?"

"Yes, it is. I made the adoption the day after you were here. Do you have another missing pet to track down?"

"No, I was going to tell you about another dog that is available but since you already adopted one I am afraid you wouldn't be interested, Helen replied"

"No, I'm afraid not, sometimes my husband feels that one dog in the house is one too many, but he is gradually growing attached to Bitsy."

"Okay, well then, I'll be on my way. Sorry to bother you, Mrs. Hebert."

Helen went to her car and sat quietly thinking for a minute before starting back to Mrs. Tolliver's house. As she approached Mrs. Tolliver's residence Helen said to herself, "I wonder what Hank is going to say when I arrive home with a new member of the family?"

About the Author

L.D. KNORR was born and raised on a dairy farm in Berks County Pennsylvania and now resides in rural Alabama. His profession as a mechanical engineer required his relocation from Pennsylvania to Mississippi, Texas, and Alabama. He honed his writing skills on engineering-related technical papers and reports. Now being retired he is focusing his attention on fiction.

He has traveled in his RV trailer with his wife Emily to visit family in Pennsylvania and Mississippi, and to wherever adventure beckons. They have been married over fifty years and were blessed with three fantastic and creative children.

www.ingramcontent.com/pod-product-compliance
Lightning Source LLC
Chambersburg PA
CBHW020611250626
47154CB00004B/1459